PRAISE: THE TIMEMATICIAN

"Wildly entertaining, with a thoughtful layer under all the villainous boasting and ka-pow action."
—*Kirkus Reviews*

"Laugh out loud funny and exquisitely painful; we are dying to know the backstory of a protagonist who demands the pronunciation of his laboratory be "la'*bore*-ah:tore-ee" because "What are we, Neanderthals? Respect the middle O!"
—*IndieReader Reviews* (5/5 rating)

"Fast and furious … with vibrant, sardonic style."
—*Foreword Reviews* (4/5 rating)

"Bereznai builds a rich world that's as zany as a funhouse and as fantastical as Star Wars."
—*Quill and Quire*

"*The Timematician* packs a powerful bionic punch as Steven Bereznai launches readers into a masterfully-created dystopian world of death beams, jet packs, knuckle blasters, and designer fembots."
—*PAX* magazine

"This tale of an underdog-turned-supervillain sucks you in and won't let you put it down until the very last page!"
—@MyBookFeatures

PRAISE: GENERATION MANIFESTATION

"Heartrending twists."
—*Foreword Clarion Reviews* (4/5 rating)

"*The Hunger Games* meets *X-Men*."
—Ryan Porter, *The Toronto Star*

"It's like the lovechild of *1984* and *The Chrysalids*."
—Joe Pedro, *Passport* magazine

"A fun, engaging read about a strong heroine fighting her way through a disturbing and unique future world."
—Todd van der Heyden, CTV News

"Action-packed from the beginning!"
—*Stefan's Books*

"Original, thrilling, and packed full of brilliant characters."
—Luke V. Marlowe, *The Page is Printed*

"Everything is written to become addicted to this story."
—*Thom Reads*

"Highly recommend."
—*Deer Tales*

"I give this story FIVE NERD glasses out of FIVE."
—*Nerd and Lace*

THE TIMEMATICIAN

Gen M: Book 2

STEVEN BEREZNAI

Jambor Publishing

FAST. FUN. FIERCE.

Cover by Demented Doctor Design

ISBN 978-1-989055-06-9 (paperback)

ISBN 978-1-989055-03-8 (ebook)

Distributed by Independent Publishers Group

Names: Bereznai, Steven, author.
Title: The timematician : a Gen M novel / Steven Bereznai.
Description: Toronto : Jambor, [2022] | Series: Gen M ; book 2.
Identifiers: ISBN: 978-1-989055-06-9   (print) | 978-1-989055-03-8 (ebook)
Subjects: LCSH: Supervillains--Fiction. | Women superheroes--Fiction. | Time travel--Fiction. | Cyborgs--Fiction. | Popular culture--Fiction. | Genetic screening--Fiction. | Good and evil--Fiction. | Genetics--Fiction. | Dystopias--Fiction. | Young adult fiction. | LCGFT: Bildungsromans. | Science fiction. | Dystopian fiction. | Apocalyptic fiction. | Action and adventure fiction. | Romance fiction. | Graphic novels.
Classification: LCC: PR9199.4.B4695 T56 2022 | PS8553.E6358 | DDC: 813/6--dc23

For Joey, my crystal queen.

Special thanks to my mom for her always insightful edits.

"I'm not going to live by their rules anymore."
—Weatherman Phil Connors, *Groundhog Day*

"Silence, you ninny!"
—Dr. Smith, *Lost in Space*

Part I

Chapter 1

My name is Doctor BetterThan—as in, I'm better than him, her, zir, and them. I've had many monikers over my multifarious existences—Professor N, Mister Know, Herr Intellekt—to name a few. During each iteration, I've had a chance to perfect my look, persona, and *modus operandi*. I've made this decimated planet quake, literally and figuratively, from the DNA regulars in the concrete tenements of the boroughs to the Supergenic elite in their shiny towers on Jupitar Island.

Forget Gen M. I'm Gen Me.

All of it has brought me to this.

Today, I destroy what's left of the world. It's been a long times coming.

I'm dressed for the occasion. My techno-armor's golden grandiosity pays homage to what past eras thought the future might look like. A double-cylinder rocket pack strapped to my back is ready for takeoff; a belt of weaponized red pods glints threateningly about my waist; in my chest plate, a glowing disc surrounded by ornamental gears pulses with pomp and power.

Geometric patterns highlight the intertwined sheathing of my battle suit's arms, legs, and torso, all molded to imply a rugged physique. Rivets glint and tasseled golden epaulets create the illusion of broad shoulders. It's industrial revolution meets high art. My most recent feature is a heating pad that eases the pain in my malformed right leg.

"*Forma occurat officium*," I say proudly. Form meets function.

The fools of this world *will* see my greatness—then I shall kill them.

I assume a haughty stance as I turn to the giant circular window that dominates the grand chamber of my ocean lair. From the center of the window's thick glass, massive clock hands point outward. Their golden shine matches that of the Roman numerals around the circumference. The ancient integer-style fell from favor long ago, but its elegant geometry shall make a triumphant return once I am the master of this world.

I gaze beyond the near-impervious pane, at white-capped waves that stretch as far as I can see. Usually, I find the waves' repetitive swoosh-slap echo soothing. Not today; too much is at stake.

I flip open an antiquated chronometer known as a "pocket watch." In my youth, I was so proud to have a wrist-strap model; that was before I realized it was crass compared to the elegance of a handheld.

The anachronistic device counts down.

My enemies are E-minus five minutes away. Everything *must* be perfect for their arrival.

I scrutinize the interior of my grand chamber; I affectionately refer to it as my "mad science" laboratory—pronounced la'*bore*-ah:tore-ee; not là-bra-tore-ee. What are we, Neanderthals? Respect the middle O!

I cross an ornate walkway of steel and rivets connecting two of many platforms suspended by slender cables or held aloft by art nouveau columns and arches within a giant metal and glass cube turned on one point.

The opulence and attention to design detail make it hard to

fathom that once this was a rig that sucked oil from beneath the ocean's floor to fuel DNA-regular war machines as they fought Supergenics for world domination.

Now, it's mine—reclaimed and transformed. Is that not what geniuses do?

Indeed, I've gloriously remodeled the defunct construct, recasting it in a retro-futuristic style where odes to steam technology rub shoulders with a Victorian sensibility. I know the Age of Exploration was rife with barbarism—colonialism, missionaries, slavery, genocide—and the filth!—but I can't help but romanticize the époque.

Oh, to be a cartographer or astronomer in that era, or a First Nations chief journeying to industrialized lands for the first time, or, best of all, the gentleman-scientist-explorer who uses his intellect, curiosity, and refinement to not only catalog and make sense of the world, but to invent.

That is the fantasy that inspires my abode.

Despite the huge window, the lighting is perfectly controlled to create stark contrasts between areas of deep shadow and strategically angled cones of light. They turn focus toward giant oil paintings in rugged platinum frames that are symmetrically arranged on easels or hang from coiled chains at various levels about the chamber. Thick strokes of deep, dark colors depict some of the grand battles that obliterated much of the planet—from the cyborg uprising in Paris to General Mave's last stand to the Great Exodus as the genetically gifted from around the world fled their human families to found their own island state.

Sadly, I was born after the genetically discordant factions forged a tentative peace.

No matter; I'll soon finish the good, apocalyptic work they started.

"And I shall do so with panache," I murmur. In no time, a new painting will join the others, the most glorious of them all—me, triumphant.

"They're almost here!" I shout. "Places everyone!"

My jetpack flares, carrying me past a glowing, revolving simulacrum of the solar system; it casts light and gorgeous shadows on dozens of tiered platforms connected by swooping ramps, angular catwalks, and spiral staircases of burnished copper.

I pass a platform where cathodes crackle with bursts of electricity; on another dais, a trio of compression tanks fitted with rotating gears release gusts of steam through whistling pipes; on a third, a charcoal, rubber polymer skin is laid out atop a marble slab like a deflated cadaver awaiting autopsy.

Exquisite! I think with glee.

Beneath my flying feet, my dutiful robots whirl and rove with spray bottles and rags, spritzing and polishing already spotless tubes and knobs one last time.

Each unit is identically dressed in a long-tail black metal jacket to imbue them with a loyal butler look. Slender shafts connect their bulbous black bodies to uni-wheels that track perfectly on the polished floors and ramps; neckless heads are equipped with 360-degree sensors within faces of featureless frosted glass; transparent craniums showcase interconnected pistons and cogs—a decorative facade that hides brains made of sophisticated circuits and microchips beneath.

"Not a speck of dust!" I remind them.

I land on the largest platform in the center of the cube and stand before a pair of marble hyperboloids, one stacked on top of the other. Mechanical arms jut around the top, holding a bevy of monitors with curved edges. Input/output ports, fluttering needle gauges, and nature-chaos icons circumnavigate the geometric construct's midsection, along with a dizzying array of toggles, switches, and dials that tease me with silent siren calls, begging me to flick and press them.

It's my master control board. I slide my fingers along it in admiration.

My lead robot rolls to my side. She's the queen of this hive. I, of course, am the king; nay! Emperor Sultan! Her design is much like the rest of my automated army, but I've gendered her with a higher-pitched voice box, a white bouffant wig with ringlets, a metallic dress that hangs like a bell around her seemingly corseted waist, bouffant shoulders and sleeves to give her a headmistress air, and, for a touch of elegance, lacy, white metalwork over her ample bosom. Most importantly, she wears a jeweled, magnetic broach in the shape of a rose on the upper left quadrant of her torso.

The bot blips and beeps at me, her flat face pulsing gently in multicolored patterns, communicating in an audio-visual language I created.

"Indeed," I agree.

She's the only one of my bots to get a name—Genetrix. It's derived from one of the old tongues that are all but forgotten. I'm self-taught from dusty books and decaying data archives. Growing up, I thought that throwing in bits of fancy talk would give me a roguish quality my classmates would ooh and aah over. As with the application of many skills in the spheres of adolescent sociability, I miscalculated. No one understood me or even tried—which prepared me well for adulthood.

"The fools of this world had no use for me," I say aloud, "well, the feeling is mutual."

Genetrix bleeps in a womp-womp way.

"Genetrix," I chide, "sarcasm is the refuge of the inferior."

I know she's being sarcastic—a deplorable and cruel form of irony that's somehow crept into her code—because an inverted question mark pulses on her face. Genetrix bleeps in response.

"Well, people *should* like know-it-alls," I answer, "*because* we know it all."

I snap my fingers to preemptively silence the bot.

"What's that smell?" I ask.

I sniff the air, which is pumped with the hypoallergenic scent of baked bread to camouflage the underlying taint of unrefined petrol soaked into the rig's bones. I thought I'd finally eliminated the noxious odor. Genetrix bleeps in a "here we go again" kind of way.

"I am *not* being O.C.D.," I insist. "Why must everything be a diagnosis with you?"

Is the bot right? Am I imagining the scent? If it's real, will my guests notice?

The proximity alarm sounds; through the window, I spy a fast-approaching hovercraft.

I turn to my *dominus imperium*—my master controls around the hyperboloids; I ignore the nature chaos commands, denoted by symbols like 🔥, 🌱, and ⚡. They are mere children's toys compared to what I have in store. I focus on the most exquisite button of them all, the red one labeled ☠.

I can't wait to press it! The looks on my enemies' faces—the horror, the humility, the recognition that I, Doctor BetterThan, beat them!—will make my years of trials worth it.

I look at my timepiece—thirty seconds to go.

Chapter 2

"**H**elmet!" I bark.

A drone wheels over, beeping as it places the helm over my head.

Genetrix bloops a compliment.

Finally, an encouraging word. She's so withholding sometimes.

"Thank you," I reply as the collar clicks and seals with a hiss. "I do look ready for victory."

The cranial gear is loaded with tech—laser goggles that also adjust light tones to lower intensities, audio enhancers and mollifiers for eavesdropping or mitigating harsh noises, filters against poison gas and atmospheric allergens, particularly pollen and animal dander.

For intimidating grandeur, gleaming Viking horns rise at the ears; tusks stretch around the mandibles, and a metallic goatee sprouts from the chin. Genetrix attaches a series of magnetic war medals to my chest.

"Thank you," I say, inclining my head. "I almost forgot."

She clucks encouragingly, and I feel warm inside. I've been

meaning to streamline her personality algorithms so she's not so critical or bossy, but perhaps I'll hold off for a few days.

I pat the medals proudly then stroke the metal goatee. These details bring me joy, so they stay—unlike the population of what's left of the planet.

I look at my golden timepiece; my fingers tighten.

"Five seconds!" I shout.

I barely breathe as I gaze at my array of monitors. On one is a visual of my moon-base death ray; it looks like an enormous mounted pen with a trio of radar dishes lined up at the tip. Another screen shows Supergenics in Jupitar City dressed in outlandish outfits; some fly, others glow. They drink bio-crafted lattes and tap pocket communicators to post to their public-ranking accounts. A third monitor lets me spy on the DNA regulars in the brutalist boroughs. They board trains bound for factories, farms, and fisheries to provide food and goods to their superpowered betters.

The fools have no idea these are the last moments of their paltry lives.

I turn my attention to the monitors showing the approaching hovercraft from various angles; it gets closer, closer …

Right on time, all of my security feeds blip out, filling with static.

"Showtime," I wheeze with glee.

My robots' flat faces flash a gentle, pastel red; their bleeps reach a fevered pitch, just within my tolerance range as they near the end of the countdown. I look at my pocket watch.

"Four, three," I say, joining in.

Genetrix bleeps a command. In response, half of my servants transform, pieces of their mechanized bodies flipping or rotating to form canons. Genetrix and the rest of my minions pull blasters from their bulbous torsos and aim at the eastern wall.

I grip the metal railing that surrounds the circular dais on which the hyperboloid master controls are located, and my lungs burn as I hold my breath for the final two seconds.

The wall blows open, and my hero guests burst inside. A muscled, blue-skinned man with a silver mohawk and red eyes all over his face fires webbing into a pair of my bot canons and, with a yank, smashes them together. An orange-haired woman with a lariat releases electricity from her palm into half a dozen of my blaster-bearing minions, frying their motherboards. A gender-neutral Supergenic swirling with magma reduces a score of my mechanical army to heaps of molten slag. A trio of DNA regulars in form-fitting black webbing and helmets with visors fly in using anti-grav belts (so dull compared to my rocket pack!) and blast my robots with ballistic rifles.

I see all of this on a holo display inside my helmet.

Their leader is a pale, female-gendered protector who wields a deadly katana and bears a graffiti-style red bird insignia on her chest. She has a ridiculous call sign that I will never utter, and her birth name brings bile to my throat. In another life, we were acrimonious classmates; now we are to-the-death nemeses.

"Your day is done, Doctor *Worse*Than!" she shouts.

My holographic display includes a social-ometer—a device of my own brilliant creation, appropriately adapted from the most sophisticated of lie-detector tech. Given the inscrutable layers of human communication, most of what people say ranges from misdirection at best to outright deceit.

Case in point. My default assumption is that my nemesis' failure to call me by my chosen name is an error on her part—like most bullies, she's more bluster than smarts—but she's also a frustratingly indirect communicator.

Hence, I've calibrated my suit's sensors to measure a bevy of tells, from heart rate to synapses firing to tonality, feeding them through a calibrator to do what I can not—read the dense substrata of nonverbal human discourse. From what I've observed, most people have a meter such as this organically built into their brains —bunch of cheaters. I shouldn't have to lower myself to their level —and soon, I shall not—but for now, the protector's words make my artificial social-ometer gently pulse with a pair of symbols—∀ (authenticity) and ¿ (sarcasm).

I grit my teeth. In one short sentence, she's unnecessarily mixed these two diametrically opposed intentions, yet *I'm* the villain? With that being the socially accepted norm, humanity doomed itself long before I came along. To help them, I once dispersed a truth gas into the atmosphere to get everyone to say what they actually meant, but due to an unforeseen chemical reaction, the field test turned the subjects into flesh-eating zombies that couldn't stop sharing the most intimate details about themselves as they split skulls and ate brains. Oh, well.

"Music!" I command.

"♪ I'm still standing …" comes from my bots' audio emitters. I prefer opera, but I've been known to whistle along to a pop tune or two. Besides, of the songs I've tried on this group, this one has proven the most distracting to them and the most centering for me.

My enemies predictably strive to attack me all at once, but my robots swarm and separate them. Divide and conquer—classic Doctor BetterThan.

"Activate execution pattern omega!" I bark.

My armor comes to life, moving me with the grace of a dancer and the ferocity of a wolverine. The blue-skinned man punches the nearest robot through its skull and fires webs at me. I'm more than ready; I grab a handful of red discs from my belt and toss them with a disdainful flick of the wrist. The first two saucers deflect his sticky bombardment; I avert my eyes as the remaining three smash into his face, chest, and hips. My audio mollifiers dim the sound of his bones breaking. He collapses in a weeping, twitching heap. I distract myself from the gruesome sight by focusing on my song—and my next target.

"♪ I'm still standing …" I sing, landing on the platform where the fiery Supergenic's glowing fists turn three of my bots into molten slag. I easily dodge a trio of magma blasts thrown my way. Ze stomps a diminutive foot, and my entire base quakes. Ze's calling forth a volcano from the ocean's depths; zirs name—Seisma —is duly earned, but so is mine.

"Not today," I murmur.

My gauntlets fire a stream of dense white foam into the "hero's" chest, smashing Seisma into a marble worktable. Dripping bubbles, ze falls to hands and knees, grunts, and struggles to get up. The Supergenic's palms glow red hot—until I unleash another round of froth that forms a sticky glob around zirs hands. Seisma tries to shake it off. The more ze struggles, the more the substance spreads, coiling around zirs arms and shoulders.

"Get it off!" Seisma shrieks.

The foam drips to the platform ze's standing on, bubbles onto Seisma's toes, crawls up zirs ankles and legs, slowly extinguishing any hint of magma under ivory froth. My enemy's power sputters and smokes like a dying volcano.

In moments, the flame-retardant foam encases my lava-empowered assailant. The suffocating cocoon becomes a coffin.

As one foe chokes to death, I prepare for the next. The orange-haired woman who sparks with electricity blasts free of the bots trying to detain her, uses her lariat to swing from her platform to mine, and lands several measures from me. She lashes her cord around my neck. If I resist, the thin coil will grow tighter, choking me even through my armor.

Wait for it, I order myself into stillness.

The woman's hands crackle, sending thousands of volts of electricity through the wire.

"You're a disgrace to all of Gen M!" she shouts as the energy surge hits me.

She pauses, no doubt expecting me to spasm and beg for mercy. Instead, I gloat at her slowly lowering jaw. Even I don't need the gently pulsing ☡ on my social-ometer to know *she's* the one experiencing a shock as my armor greedily sucks up the gigawatts she's funneling through her lasso.

"Gen M is nothing," I snort. "I am all!"

Genetrix chortles proudly in agreement. I beam.

The Supergenic gasps—I'd like to think in awe of my words, but as my social-ometer flashes Ω, I know she is in excruciating pain.

"Social-ometer off!" I order.

Genetrix bleeps questioningly.

"Because I said so," I hiss at her under my breath. "Just let me do it my way."

I turn back to the orange-haired interloper. I wrap my hand around the cord extending from her hands to my neck. My fingers squeeze, and she gasps as my armor not only absorbs the energy she's sending through the conduit, but forcefully sucks the terawatts from her.

"Hurts," she stammers. "Please, stop."

My audio mufflers fade her words to a soft drone.

I yank on the lariat, pulling her off her feet. She thunks hard to her knees. She struggles to let go of the cord, but as my suit draws more and more electricity from her, the suctioning electro-voltaic forces fuse her fingers to the filament.

Steam rises from her orange flesh. Blood drips from her nose and evaporates into red mist as her atrophying muscles convert to electricity. Her orange flesh turns a mummified grey, vacuuming inward like a drink box sucked dry, reducing her to a withered, smoking husk.

The lariat sparks twice, dims to a dull sheen, and releases my neck. My fingers open; free of my grip, the filament recoils and smacks into its owner with such force her cadaver bursts into dusty chunks.

"Next!" I cry.

The two male protectors fire their ballistic weapons, felling a cadre of my bots. One has a crow sigil on his impressive chest; the other, a hummingbird. The black compression fabric of their form-fitting uniforms shows off their muscled physiques, making me keenly aware that they don't need the illusion of athleticism that my armor creates for me; I'm reminded that pre-adolescent precursors to men like these were one of many banes of my youth.

Genetrix beeps next to me in a gossipy way.

"No," I snort derisively, glancing at the woman with the katana, slicing and dicing bot after bot. "I *can't* believe she's dating both of them." It's not a new conversation.

Genetrix whistles sensually.

"Language," I chide, not disagreeing.

My rocket pack propels me onto another platform with a clearer sightline to and from the katana woman. The pair of muscled men fly after me and fire repeatedly.

They're good enough for her? I wonder for the millionth time, deflecting armor-piercing bullets with fluid karate chops. *But all she ever granted me was attitude?*

Long gone are the days when I could assuage myself with assurances that she's simply a lone wolf, even if she seems more comfortable fighting on her own three platforms away rather than side-by-side with the two men who share her bed.

All at once? I wonder.

Her paramours aim their rifles and fire at close range. Their bullets bounce off my cuirass. I smack one of their rifles, and it flies over the dais. I grab the barrel of the other protector's firearm and bend it 90 degrees.

They look at each other and clench their fists. In previous confrontations, I've underestimated the pair. They have no superpowers, so what hope do they have against me? Yet, as I've learned to my dismay, they are more dangerous than the Supergenics I've just felled.

The latter have been told they are special all their lives and think themselves all-mighty. In their hubris, they underestimate me and overestimate themselves, making them easy to isolate, neutralize, and extinguish. Not so these fellows. As much as my bots have tried to separate them, they've worked in tandem to stick together. Their assault is equally coordinated.

Sharp spikes cover Crow's knuckles. He punches me repeatedly —across the jaw, sternum, and solar plexus. He's strong for a DNA regular. The spikes scratch and dent my armor, and my head rattles inside my helmet. Hummingbird's the sneakier and quicker of the two. As Crow distracts and throws me off balance, Hummingbird stabs a sizzling energy blade into the supports of my bum leg.

They wait for me to fall. If I were wearing my old armor, the blade would've severed the brace and cut through my knee. Hummingbird looks at his knife, crumpled on itself, crackling pathetically.

"I've made some upgrades," I explain. "Brains best brawn." They pant, bird sigils rising up and down on their flexed chests.

"*Rusus mea*," I say. The pair turn their visored gazes to each other and shrug in a way I've seen many times before. They don't understand.

"My turn," I translate. They're the last words they'll hear.

Their biceps bunch as they prepare for another assault, but I'm on a schedule. I grab the tops of their helmets, dig my fingers in, cracking their visors with my thumbs, and rip the helmets from their heads. Even with the streaks of grey in their black hair and lines about their eyes, both are boyishly handsome with naturally tan skin. Crow has freckles across the bridge of his nose.

Genetrix whistles a catcall.

"Yes," I agree, "she has a type."

They twist, leverage their weight to break my grip, and the instant they're free, they pounce. I catch them by their throats and lift them off their feet. They sputter and choke.

"Fret not," I assure them. "You are the vanguard of many more dead to come. *Electricae!*"

The energy I absorbed from the electricity-generating Supergenic discharges from my armor, out of my hands, and into them. They scream and convulse. My internal buffers mute their horrible cries and fuzz out the image of their suffering, but I still hear *her*.

"No!" katana woman shouts. She remained stoic and silent as I

16

felled the Supergenics. They were her unlikely allies, so their deaths barely touched her cold heart. But even with my social-ometer turned off, I see how much these two mean to her.

"*Affirmativa*," I insist, releasing the men's smoldering charcoal bodies. They thud to the dais. I flick my armored fingers to free them of ash. Genetrix spritzes each of my gauntlets with window cleaner and rubs them clean with paper towels.

Meanwhile, the last woman standing cuts a swathe through my bots. Her blade is made of a magnificent alloy that dices their metal hides and forcefields with equal ease. I look forward to adding it to my collection.

Hip jets propel her upward. I grin as she gets closer.

"*Unum plus*," I murmur.

One more.

She lands before me and predictably throws a trio of stars stamped with black graffiti birds that I easily dodge. They sever a hose feeding into a compression tank on a neighboring platform, releasing a purple gas that hisses all about me. She fires her photon gun; the ray ignites the vapor, engulfing me in flames. I pause within the inferno, to let her think she's harmed me. If I were wearing my previous set of armor, I'd be screaming in agony as the hyper-hot substance burned through me. My audio projectors emit fake sounds of me suffering.

And then, I float free, unscathed within my updated suit. My enemy grunts.

"Social-ometer," I say, "on."

It pulses with a colon and an open chevron bracket—the symbol that tells me she's surprised. I smirk in satisfaction. I never get tired of seeing that.

She swings her katana in a dizzying pattern that even a predictive algorithm has no hope of countering. Yet, I easily dodge, duck, and jump; her katana whistles a breath from my helm. It's almost as if I know her every move before she makes it. The thought borders on sarcasm, but I'll allow it.

I grab her wrist, crush it with a single squeeze, and she drops her weapon. My fingers close about her throat and lift her off her feet just as I did with her beaus.

"You were a fool to defy the genius of Doctor BetterThan!" My laugh is a wheeze inside my helm, but my voice modulator releases it as a drawn-out gush of maniacal laughter.

I wait for her absurd response. I do so love knowing what's about to happen. The power, the control, the—

"She was right," the protector says as my grip tightens. "I should've listened to her. Next time, I will."

I pause. Did I mishear?

"That's not your line," I reply. "You always say, 'you are but one, and we are many. We will stop you.' Then we battle as only arch-enemies can."

"Not this time," she says.

Is she mocking me? I wait for my social-ometer to flash the beta symbol for belittlement. Instead, the holo light flares ∀. She means every word of her threat, and she believes them to be true. She speaks as if she knows my secret. But that can't be, can it?

"And how do you plan to stop the great Doctor BetterThan?" I demand.

"There's only one way for you to find out," she says.

I prepare for her to snap my hold with a twisting backflip; instead, her jaw clenches, and her teeth grind.

"What are you—"

My words die as she convulses.

"*Deodamnatus*," I swear. "Genetrix, the anti-toxin!"

Genetrix's decapitated head beeps at me from the floor.

Froth bubbles over the protector's lips.

"Revolting," I say. I release her corpse, and my rocket pack flares, flying me back several paces. She thuds on the platform next to her dead lovers. I pick up the window cleaner Genetrix dropped and give my armored palms a second spritz.

Genetrix chirps at me like a scolding nanny.

"Of course, I know that pathogens can't get through my battle suit!" I snap—at least no germ that I know of. No point in taking chances.

As if she's reading my mind, the bot squawks disparagingly.

"I can hear you," I say. "Honestly, stop micromanaging my feelings."

I kneel next to the protector's dead body.

"You must be wondering how I've always been three steps ahead of you," I say. At the risk of being a cliché, I can't help monologuing. It's so satisfying!

"You all believe it's my tech genius that makes me a threat. Fools. I do accept the mantle of technius, but it is *not* my technical prowess that makes me an enhanced being. Mastering all this," I gesture at my laboratory, "took a long time—a long *times*, to be precise." I tap my temple. "If only you knew my power."

Sweat beads my brow. The way katana woman spoke with her dying breath, *did* she know? Genetrix bleeps at me impatiently.

"Yes, I'm still going through with it," I insist. I'd chide her, but she's right. Best get on with it.

My finger traces an intricate pattern on my cuirass, and a compartment in the chest armor opens, revealing what the untrained eye might take to be an archaic golden key with a fanciful rendition of a plague mask on one end and a trio of prongs on the other. In truth, it's the most sophisticated network activator ever devised. I slide it into an ornate key slot on my control panel and twist.

The words *DEATH RAY ONLINE* flash on a rounded monitor.

I hold my palm above the giant red button labeled with a skull-and-crossbones.

"Goodbye, humanity," I say.

My hand slams downward—until the protector's final proclamation replays in my mind. *She was right. I should've listened to her. Next time, I will.*

My fingers freeze a breath from the kill switch.

"Do it!" I order myself. I try to force my hand onto the activator button.

A vertical line of orange light moves across Genetrix's flat face.

"Don't you roll your eyes at me!"

Genetrix whistles.

"You don't understand," I snap. "You *never* understand. Don't you see? I'm a genius. My gift *is* my curse. I can't let the protector's words go. I *have* to know." I take a trembling breath. "One more time, Genetrix. One more time to solve this mystery, and then I *will* end them."

Genetrix bleeps her version of "OK" in a drawn-out, skeptical tone.

"You won't even remember this unless I choose to program it into you," I say. "This time, I'm not going to."

I close my eyes and mentally reach inward. A casual observer might think that I was meditating. But while I'm entering into an altered state, one that could arguably be called transcendental, meditative is not how I would describe the experience that is about to unfold.

Through a combination of breathwork, visualizations, and heightened emotions, I've learned to flick a switch in my brain— one that makes me more Generation Manifestation than I'd care to admit.

Here we go again, I think as I envision a master control panel before me. The monitors show various memories, a veritable slew of high- and low-lights from my life. I imagine myself holding an ornate key with a butterfly design at the end. Its wings flutter softly. I insert it into the imaginary control panel within, turn the key, and a monitor flashes the words *QUANTUM SINGULARITY ONLINE*.

A rainbow button appears with an hourglass on it.

"*Nunc futuri*," I sigh. I slam the button. A moment of pure stillness surrounds me. This is the worst part, like being at the top of a roller coaster the instant before it goes over the edge.

I brace myself. It didn't help when my mom forced me onto the rickety wooden ride at the annual fair, and it doesn't help now.

The vortex opens and sucks my essence downward, upward, and outward—all at once, ricocheting me through my past. I experience the battle that's just unfolded, but in reverse. The antiseptic I spritzed onto my metal palms goes back into the bottle; katana woman's dead body flies into my hand; the froth at her lips dissolves into her mouth; her jaw un-chews her hidden poison pellet. She's alive.

That's far enough, I think. All I have to do is stop her from poisoning herself, and I can get the answers I seek.

I try to halt the rewind, but my power's a rollercoaster in more ways than one—without the safety bar, car, or track. I overshoot where I want to stop, and the backflash accelerates, rewinding the events that have just transpired more quickly.

I release katana woman and float backward through roaring flames; the flames revert into purple gas as her blast shoots out of it and into her pistol; the indigo haze retracts into the tubes; the tubes reform, and the throwing stars return to her hand. It's almost too fast for me to follow.

No, no, no!

I mentally squeeze, and with a jarring snap, unseen quantum bands yank my psyche out of the backflash, slamming me into my past physical self.

I blink rapidly, pant, and wipe the sweat from my brow.

I look at the pocket watch in my hand then stare out the window of my cubic grand chamber as my enemies' hovercraft races toward me.

Chapter 3

"**H**elmet!" I bark.

A drone bleeps, places the protective covering of tusks and horns over my head, then I fly to my master control panel.

"Five seconds!" I shout.

My robots chirp in anticipation. They have no recollection of what's just happened. My anomalous brain remembers everything; their mechanized ones do not.

I focus my attention on the monitor showing the eastern exterior wall of my cubic chamber where my foes will blast their way in.

The hovercraft is getting closer, closer …

As per always, and by that, I mean every time I've gone through this attack, which is numerous, all of my security feeds go out. My monitors fill with static.

"Let's get this over with," I mutter.

My robots' faces flash red; their bleeps grow louder, and even though they're attenuated to not overstimulate my senses, the sound is like needles in my brain. The protector will pay for riling me up like this.

"Mute!" I shout, and they go silent.

I don't bother looking at my pocket watch. My mechanized minions pull blasters from their bulbous torsos and obey their programming, aiming at the eastern wall.

I drum my fingers next to the button labeled with the skull and crossbones. Genetrix senses my impatience and rubs my back soothingly. Sensors in my armor transmit her touch as comforting warmth. The countdown reaches zero. I step away from Genetrix and stare at the eastern wall.

Nothing happens.

"They're late," I exhale with annoyance. Genetrix's sing-song whistle goes up and down. My eyes widen.

"You're right," I agree. "That means—"

The *western* wall explodes, throwing me off my feet. My metal epaulets make deep gouges as I slide along a catwalk. Support cables snap and the suspended walkway tips, throwing me over the edge. My rocket pack sputters, too slow to activate, and I smash into the shiny marble floor. A bot helps me to my feet; I shove it away.

My head snaps to the left as my attackers fly through the hole they've created in the *wrong* wall.

"*Damnare!*" I curse.

Jet belts propel the two muscular male protectors and the athletic katana woman into my lair, all of them in uniforms of tight black webbing with bird sigils on their chests. Their superpowered allies follow—the orange-haired electricity woman, the non-binary with pulsing skin of magma, and the muscled blue man with a silver mohawk and red eyes all over his head.

The present has changed.

Did I butterfly effect myself? I wonder, inadvertently making one alteration to the timeline, which then created another unintended variation, and another, cascading beyond my control?

No, I realize. I didn't travel back far enough or have any interactions or course changes that could disrupt the timeline—which means, I'm dealing with something far worse.

I recall the katana-wielding protector's final words—*She was right. I should've listened to her. Next time, I will.*

This isn't my first time repeating this battle. That's how I know so much of what will happen—and how to counter it. The protector ought to have no memory of those other timelines, including the one just past; somehow, she does—and she's making different decisions. Which means I've lost my greatest advantage. Now, anything can happen.

While her compatriots work together to tear through my robots with bolts of lightning, webbing, lava blasts, and blasters, the protector with the katana comes for me, belt jets blasting her upward. She pulls the katana from the sheathe on her back and slices her way through my mechanized minions.

"How does it feel not knowing what comes next?" she asks.

Awful, I'm about to reply—until my social barometer flashes Ⴎ. She's being rhetorical.

I fire ten laser beams from my knuckle blasters; her whirling katana deflects them into my robots; their blips turn shrill, cutting out as their operating systems go offline. Genetrix falls.

The protector lands on a neighboring dais and throws her battle stars; the stamped bird insignia on each twirling weapon glitters amber. The stars miss me—Ha!—and fly by either side of my horned helm. The weapons' sharp, curved tips thud into my master controls.

With that kind of incompetence, maybe it doesn't matter if she's aware of my do-overs. Victory shall still be mine.

My robots close in on her. She flips, rolls, evades, and guts them one by one.

Genetrix's head lies at my feet. She bleeps.

"Agreed," I say. "This is not ideal." As much as my battles with katana woman are electrifying, I dare not wait for her to reach my side. She may have missed with her throwing stars, but she's unerring with that blade.

I shove my ornate plague mask key into its slot on the control panel and turn. Gears activate and click. A rounded monitor flashes the words *DEATH RAY ONLINE*.

Katana woman's hip rockets blast her up and over; she lands a few measures from me. I slam my hand toward the giant red ☠ button. She snags my wrist with a thin, silver coil; I try to send electricity through it, but it's non-conducting. Like me, she's learned from our previous encounter.

She should not remember! I rage.

She yanks me from the doomsday switch and off my feet, armor and all. She always was a brute. I make a note to add gravity plating to the soles of my boots.

I land ignominiously on my chest, knocking the breath from me. She whirls her blade in a dizzying pattern, slicing and dicing my helmet. Horns, mandibles, and faceplate clatter to the floor. She raises her visor. My gaze darts up and to the right to avoid meeting hers.

"Still can't look anyone in the eye?" she asks.

I *won't* be made fun of for that. I'm at her feet, but my chin tilts imperiously, and my nose lifts as if *I* were towering over *her*.

"*Ultimo finum ludum,*" she snorts.

Ultimate end game.

My eyes narrow. How dare she use Latin against me!?

She raises her sword, ready to strike.

"*Iterum,*" I growl.

One more time.

I don't care if she can remember bits of this timeline—it won't be enough to stop me. This is *my* power. I turn the rewind key in my brain and brace for the stomach-wrenching reset. Nothing happens.

"You're not going anywhere," she says. The last of my bots fall. On a dais behind her, her compatriots gather—the trio of Supergenics and her pair of lovers—and watch.

She smiles knowingly. I barely notice what's left of my social-ometer pulsing inside my shattered helmet; I'm too busy following her gaze toward the trio of throwing stars lodged in the equipment around me. The bird emblem in each star glitters with yellow crystals.

Wasn't her sigil simply stamped on the throwing stars in stark black before? The crystals aren't her style at all—too flashy and fun —and the amber tones are so outside her color scheme, I'm sure I would've remembered.

The crystals emit an envelope of waxy light that enshrouds me.

I press gently on the barrier. It gives in a gelatinous way—but doesn't break. It holds me with a warm grip that sends a chill through my armor into the depths of my bones.

This can't be good.

I shake off my doubt, remind myself who I am, and the servo motors in my armor straighten my spine to its full height.

"You think *this* can hold *me?*" I demand.

"I do," she says. "I don't get the science behind them. That's more your thing. But I'm told they're quantum stabilizers."

My brow arches. What did she say? In our youth, she struggled to grasp the basics of electromagnetic theory; now she's going on like an authority in the field of particle physics?

"I never thought I'd be desperate enough to use them," she adds. "I figured it had to be a trick, a way for her to escape or to get me killed."

My nemesis is making less sense than usual. I've indulged her and my curiosity long enough. I put the imaginary butterfly key into my mental master control panel, turn, and imagine my finger pressing a button labeled with an hourglass.

"Goodbye, Caitlin," I say, avoiding her gaze. I brace myself for a rollercoaster whoosh, a centrifugal rewind, and then—revenge!

Nothing happens. I remain in the present, encapsulated by yellow jello. I shake my head.

Concentrate! I berate myself.

"One moment," I tell her sternly.

Her arm arcs outward. "By all means."

26

My temples and arms clench as I try to activate my power again. I open my eyes.

"Are you done?" she asks.

Sweat soaks my brow and runs down my back. Why did I put that stupid heating pad around my leg? It's boiling in here! In contrast, she coolly balances a throwing star on one finger like a vaudeville performer. The weapon glitters with yellow crystals.

"I've barely begun!" I shout. Internally, I'm jamming that impotent hourglass button over and over. Why isn't it working? Why am I not in the past finding a way to fix this?

From the corner of my eye, I see her toss the star into the air, catch it behind her back, and then hold it in front of her, contemplating the glinting yellow crystals. "Since time's still moving forward, I guess this stuff works."

Her words make my averted gaze widen in horrified understanding.

I'm trapped!

I look to my robots for rescue; she and her allies have reduced them to scrap.

No! I rage. *No, no, no!*

A blaster flicks out of my forearm armor. I point it at her time-stabilizing tech. Her katana whistles in the air, passes the yellow barrier as if it weren't there, and slices the blaster in half. It sparks, bounces on the dais, and falls over the edge.

"I didn't believe her," the protector says, "not for the longest of times. I mean, super strength and teleportation are one thing, but time travel? Everyone knows that's nonsense. But she taught me to strengthen the part of the mind responsible for déjà vu. Turns out that whatever you've got in your brain, it's just an extreme form of a quantum sensitivity that many of us have."

I snort then laugh. "Listen to you, blathering with *such* authority. You don't know a gluon from a boson!"

"Yet here we are," she says, sharpening her already impossibly sharp katana on one of the tusks she sliced from my helmet.

"Here we are indeed," I scoff. "You think you're so smart, so clever, so much better than me because you think you've beaten me at my own game."

"I mean," she shrugs, "kind of."

"Well, the jest is on you," I insist. I close my eyes, and with all my will, I activate my power.

I open my eyes. The protector looks at me questioningly. "Are you constipated? Fiber's your friend."

"It irritates my gut!" I stomp my foot.

I can't let her outsmart me nor have the last word; *I'm* the genius! The quantum sensitivity she spoke of, I've encountered it before, if rarely and with little consequence. Some people will have a fleeting sense that they are experiencing a do-over. In theory, this provides them with an opportunity to make a new, different decision. But the moment is so ephemeral, and people are such (pathetic) creatures of habit, even if they have a premonition, a 'gut feeling' of what's to come, they rarely turn east when they've previously gone west. Even those that do make a change, who cares? They, their actions, their lives, their deaths are so insignificant, it matters not.

Until now.

The truth of my predicament hits me full force. I throw myself at the barrier and slam my hands against it.

"Let me out of here!" I squeal. "Let me out let me out let me out! I am Doctor BetterThan! You *will* grovel before me! You will ..."

The gooey barrier catches my hands and jerks me off balance. I fall into its sticky embrace. I trash, becoming more enmeshed.

"I won't ever be able to time-travel," the protector sighs.

"Jealous?" I demand. The goo's become a straitjacket, pinning my arms around my torso.

"Yes," she admits without reservation. "But I am getting better at catching glimpses of my own futures as they would've been before you reversed things. That's something."

Her voice is as grating as when we were kids.

"That?" I yell. "That is nothing. That is less than nothing. It's vermin in the place of foie gras; it's—"

"It was enough to beat you—with help," she admits. "Not all of us are born with superpowers. Some of us have to work to be special. That's what makes *me* Gen M. With guidance, I trained my temporal grey matter until I could remember as much as I needed to finally convince me of the truth." My nemesis stops sharpening her sword and holds up the star with the yellow crystals. "I should've used these the last time we fought, but I still wasn't convinced I could trust her or her gadgets. She's the one person on this planet who may be more conniving than you."

"Who is *she*?" I demand. Of course, Caitlin has an accomplice; she couldn't pull this off on her own. But who? Who could've figured it out? Who could've given her such tech?

"It was Bradie's idea to talk with her," my enemy says, looking over to her paramours. They've taken off their helmets.

"It takes a villain to stop a villain," the one with the freckles and crow sigil says.

I *hate* him! I fight the guck around me, determined to rip out his throat. The substance tightens around my thrashing form.

"Maybe you'll meet her," my nemesis muses, pressing the tip of her katana to my Adam's apple, "in The Asylum."

My sweat runs cold, my bladder constricts, and I stop struggling.

The Asylum.

My lower lip quivers. I'd rather die than go there. I feel the sharp of her weapon against my soft skin. Do I dare shove myself onto her blade and truly end it all? No more resets. The final pause. She seems to read my mind—curse her and her acuity!—and she pulls the blade a measure away.

"I still remember how you were in school," she says.

"Silence!" I shout. Without the voice modulator in my helmet, it comes out a shriek.

"I never would've guessed this is who you would turn into," she continues. "With your power, you could've made such a difference, warned us of disasters to come, guided leaders who'd made decisions misguided by ignorance or arrogance, helped us be our best selves."

"Spare me the Gen M propaganda," I say.

But I wonder, *Could she be right? Was there a better way? Might I have left my isolated ocean base to join humanity rather than destroy it?*

"Never!" In a desperate fit, I twist to one side. The goo jerks back then launches me to the floor like a pellet from a slingshot. My chest plate slams into the dais. The round centerpiece above my sternum takes the brunt of the impact and starts to glow.

A jolt of turbo power runs through my armor's anti-gravity discs. They whine, fighting the goo pressing my cheek ignominiously to the floor mere digits from my nemesis' heels. My armor lifts me vertical and floats my feet off the platform. I hover above my nemesis. I prefer my jet pack—it's wonderfully grandiose—but this will do.

"Caitlin!" her male companions cry in unison as they realize I am not done, and this battle is not over. They and her other allies run up stairs and across bridges toward us.

The gears around the glowing circle in my chest plate turn, and a beam blasts outward, making the goo fly off me. My nemesis' eyes widen. Her blade turns into a blur.

My armor emits a protective energy field; her katana disrupts it and slices clean through the power booster on my chest. It crackles then goes dark. I drop, and as I do, she dices the pistons and gears that create a brace for my bad leg. I'm not sure if she's being petty or not taking any chances. I land hard; without the support for my disabled limb, I crumple to my hands and knees.

It doesn't matter. Free of the gel, I activate my power. I feel the universe stretch then compress, preparing to suck me back in time —until the amber encasing blobs around me once more. The moment it makes contact, it's like spikes being nailed through my skull, lashing me to the present. I scream as quantum forces rebound within me.

I gasp, struggle for breath, and pull at the guck. She holds her palm up to her companions, and they stop in the middle of a bridge. Her lovers fold their arms over their chests. I wheeze a laugh.

"*Perpetuum non parceres*," I mock.

She looks to the taller of her mates. Hummingbird gazes at a small monitor on his wrist. "Translator says it means, you can't hold me forever."

She sighs and looks at me. I avoid her gaze; I'm already plotting my escape—and triumphant return.

"You'll never give up," she says. "Even imprisoned, you're dangerous. All it will take is one guard screwing up, one tech failure, and you'll rewind again."

"To a time before you learned how to train your temporal sensitivity," I taunt her.

"No," she replies. "I won't let you hurt this world evers again."

Her use of the word evers—plural—is not lost on me. Is it possible that, on some level, she gets me?

She lifts the blade, ready to slice through my exposed neck.

I stare at the floor as I suck back tears and snot.

I won't beg I won't beg I won't …

I wait for my end—the seconds tick by excruciatingly slow.

What is taking so long? This is so like her!

I dare to look up, annoyance momentarily eclipsing fear. Caitlin's eyes twitch, rolling to the back of her head.

That's odd. It's almost as if—

Her trembling hands clench, then her grip goes limp; her sword blurs in my vision as it falls point first toward my face. I jerk; the katana nicks my goatee, pierces the dais, and slides through the platform down to the hilt.

I pant and tilt my head. The protector—Caitlin—has stopped trembling, and her eyes roll back into place. Avoiding her gaze, I take in her expression. I don't need a social-ometer to realize she's confused.

She stares at her sword hand; it's slowly dissolving into black ash that drifts in the air. She staggers back, hitting the railing. She stares at her other arm; it's also dissolving, right through her uniform. The sleeve slumps against her torso.

On the bridge behind her, the magma Supergenic collapses into a pile of black dust. Ze was part ash to begin with and thus is the first to go. Next, the electric Supergenic crackles with energy and solidifies into a petrified black husk.

Fascinating!

"Caitlin, what's happening?" her boyfriend with the freckles cries in panic. Hummingbird holds Crow's waist and cheek as he blubbers. "I ... I can't see!" Black dust rises from his eye sockets. Hummingbird looks ready to say something, but his jaw collapses into black motes.

"No!" Caitlin cries. She looks at me. I look away. "What have you done?"

"*Mors trabem*," I explain.

"Death beam," she translates.

On one of my rounded monitors, we see my giant blaster on the moon shooting the planet with a glowing beam that cascades outward like an expanding tidal wave. It covers the globe within minutes.

"But ... you never inserted the key," she insists. "You never pushed the button. I stopped you."

I struggle against the goo around me, grasp the hilt of her blade, pull it free of the dais, and shove the tip into the yellow crystals of the nearest throwing star embedded in my master control panel. Shattered crystal shards clatter to the platform, and a third of the goo holding me fizzles away.

"My plans have plans," I snort, regaining my sense of superiority as I slice through the remaining two stars with my vanquished enemy's weapon. The gelatinous field evaporates. I crack my neck and pick up a fallen robo stem to use as a cane. "I set a timer for my death ray—just in case."

I project utter disgust for her puny intellect for ever believing she could defeat me.

"Will you never learn?" I taunt. "I am Doctor BetterThan. Of course, I've accounted for every contingency!"

Or so I would have her believe. In truth, I'd set the auto-activation counter so many timelines ago, I'd completely forgotten, and I'd simply never traveled back far enough since to create a reset.

I chuckle. In my long, luckless lives, something finally works in my favor.

"Liar," she says.

I blink in surprise. She speaks with such authority even I catch her tone.

"I don't know what you're talking about," I insist.

"You're as surprised as I am," she insists.

How can such an idiot be so insightful? It's infuriating.

Behind her, the muscles of her two men atrophy; ash floats out of their now loose-fitting uniforms until the clingy mesh collapses like molting skin, and they are gone. She winces but swallows back any other reaction. She always was tough, way tougher than me. *It's probably why she's lasting so long, holding herself together through stubbornness and strength of will.* Her other arm is gone, but the rest of her remains—for now.

Despite our differences, I can't help feel a grudging respect. If she'd made better choices, who knows how all of this might've turned out.

"Correct," I say. It feels strange to concede that to her. She stripped me of my helmet, but it's the admission that makes me feel naked. "Many timelines ago, when I first built my death ray, I had a *discrimina conscientia.*"

"I haven't learned that term," she says.

Is she asking me to teach her? It's too little, too late, but I suppose I can be a gracious victor.

"A crisis of conscience," I say.

"You didn't know if you could go through with it," she says.

"How do you do that?" I ask.

"Do what?" she replies. Bits of black float off her lips, nose, and cheeks.

"Connect dots I didn't even know were there."

"My mom was … complicated," she explains.

"As was mine," I say. Am I enjoying this interaction as much as the victory itself?

Nonsense! I scoff.

We silently look to my bank of monitors. They're jacked into satellite cams, personal devices, and surveillance drones. As the death-cascade washes over the planet, we see the effects worldwide.

In Jupitar City, Supergenics drop bio-crafted lattes or colorful shopping bags stuffed with the latest fashions as their garish—and suddenly bodiless—ensembles flop onto café chairs or sidewalks amidst piles of ash.

In the boroughs, a security feed shows us a classroom of teens sitting at their uncomfortable desks, dressed in their Testing Day best as they wait to find out if they are DNA regular or will follow in the footsteps of Gen M. Dresses with puffed shoulders, blazers, and ties slump as their bodies disintegrate.

On an ocean fishing vessel, crew members harpoon an attacking kraken. Its crushing tentacles writhe in the air, slam the water's surface, and wrap around the ship. Kraken, crew, and their haul of giant deep-sea tuna (a kraken favorite) erupt into black dust. The empty ship bobs in the waves.

The images are mirrored in the growing lands, the Yellow Zone, and the outer colonies where pets, livestock, and wild beasts turn to black dust, from the most hideous mutated hound to a herd of cows to a rare kaleidoscope of monarch butterflies that will never reach their rehabilitated breeding ground. Forests petrify; agri-fields collapse; aqua-culture tanks turn into containers brimming with brackish sludge.

It's the flock of disintegrating shadowren that brings a tear to Caitlin's eye.

"Stop this," she says.

"It's like toothpaste," I say. "It doesn't go back in the tube."

"That's not true," she says, "not for you."

"Ah, Caitlin," I sigh, "a small part of me is going to miss you."

Her eyes widen. At least, I think they do. Her dissolving face makes it hard to say for sure. Based on facial expression cue cards I hated growing up (why can't people just say what they mean?), I think my words have given her hope. Best I clarify. "The rest of me is glad to see you and everyone else go."

"You're insane!" she shouts. "It will kill you too."

Her chatter is textbook superhero nonsense. I turn her weapon so it catches the light. "I've inoculated myself."

I take a moment to congratulate myself on making the death beam painless. Without the audio mollifiers in my broken helmet, her screams of agony would be murder on my nerves.

"It doesn't have to end this way," she insists as she continues to disintegrate. Her breasts and left hip sag. She won't last much longer. "You've proven you *are* Doctor BetterThan, better than us all. Isn't that enough?"

I ponder the question.

"You can undo this. Please," she urges. "Go back and change it."

"No," I say.

I swing the katana; it slices through the black ash of her neck. Her webbed uniform with the bird insignia crumples to the floor; a mound of charcoal forms upon it; the sheath for her katana clatters, and her helmet rolls into my foot.

My heart hammers as I take in the moment.

"I did it," I realize out loud. "I'm the only living being on the planet. I win."

Chapter 4

Within minutes of my victory, a hoverjet arrives from my offsite assembly plant, offloading a fresh battalion of robots. They cart away the remains of their fallen predecessors, vacuum the black dust of my former foes, and throw their sooty clothes into an incinerator; others repair the damage done by the so-called heroes. A 3-D printer hums as it outputs an oil painting in a thick gold frame, depicting me vanquishing my nemeses.

I have a bot put the anti-time travel throwing stars into a containment box for later study; another of my robots hands me an ornate cane adorned with an intricate silver octopus as the handle. Without my brace, I lean on it heavily.

As they proceed with their work, I turn to my master control panel and click the plague key counter-clockwise; a monitor flashes DEATH RAY OFFLINE. I pull the key free, open the door of a tubular copper cabinet, and hang the key alongside a slew more, each with a distinct design on the handle—a ruby dagger, a cog, a coiled serpent, to list a few.

I brush my finger over them, past one with a shadowren bird, and select a key with a head of lacy metalwork around a jeweled rose.

"You," I point at a passing robot, "you will be my new Genetrix."

It inclines its head and bleeps in agreement. A keyhole opens on the back of its cranium. I slide the key in, and I delight in the tactile sensation of twisting it, followed by the satisfying, musical chime of cogs turning. The robot chirps as it downloads the programming for its new role.

Its body clicks, and more cogs rotate, flipping pieces of the robot's torso in, out, and sideways, forming a bell-shaped Victorian gown around its uni-wheel. White metallic lace flows over its bosom, its shoulders and sleeves puff out, and one of its brethren rolls over to place a white, Victorian updo on the feminized bot's head and a jeweled rose broach on her now ample bosom.

My new Genetrix clucks critically at the drone models, waving dismissively for them to be away as if they were less-than-adequate salespeople at a clothing boutique that's also failing to meet her standards—as if anything could.

"Some help," I say to her with a hint of petulance, pointing at my collar where bits of my busted helmet remain attached, pressing uncomfortably into my neck.

My new Genetrix makes a chortling squawk.

"I am *not* being a big baby," I insist. Why did I program her to be this way?

She shrugs, working brusquely to get the jammed collar undone. It reminds me of my mother, years ago, none-too-gently fighting with an overly tight tie she'd bound around my neck for Testing Day.

"Careful," I snap.

Genetrix snorts condescendingly.

"Caitlin did not nearly beat me. It was all part of my plan," I lie.

Genetrix squawks, not believing a word.

"Well, I *was* victorious, wasn't I?" I reply, gesturing toward the newly printed oil painting as a pair of my drones mount it on an easel. I nod in admiration at this giant version of myself holding Caitlin's katana overhead; she, her muscled men, and the trio of supergenics lie at my feet. I gesture for my bots to move it a little to the left.

Genetrix clacks; her cold, metal knuckles dig into my neck as she gets a firm grip on the collar.

"What do you mean, 'we'll see?'" I demand.

She shrugs.

"I don't need your approval," I say. "I earned this. *Me.*"

The bot's fingers clench, and she snaps the collar with brute strength. I sigh in relief, savoring the unimpeded breath. The rest of the suit clicks, emits a hydraulic hiss, and opens. I step free, wearing a silk onesie and double socks on my feet to prevent chaffing.

Genetrix slides a red velvet robe with the initials *DB* onto my arms and over my shoulders. She claps at a pair of bots, and they strap a padded metal brace with cogs, pistons, and hydraulics around my bad leg. The mechanisms hiss pleasantly as they help me slide my toes into slippers that match the monogrammed robe. A hoverdrone bobs next to me, offering me a Twinkie on a silver tray with reconstituted lactose-free milk in a champagne glass. I stuff the Twinkie into my mouth. *Delectamenti*! I could eat these for the rest of my life—and so I shall. I raise the champagne glass to my robots.

"To victory!" I cheer.

They hold their palms to their chest plates, bleating worshipfully. I smile as the soothing symphony washes over me. Whistling in time, I slide the katana into its sheath, walk to a lift that resembles an ornate golden birdcage, and step aboard.

I slide shut its accordion door, give a circular crank three spins, then depress a button labeled 🦖. The conveyance smoothly descends past the wondrous platforms, ramps, and circular staircases of my laboratory, down through a steel-framed circular glass shaft that takes me beneath the cubular construct perched dozens of measures above the ocean.

I get a look at its polished underbelly, gleaming immaculately. I look down at the waves crashing against the frame of thick metal beams that cradle my lair. The sound of smacking water is muffled by the carriage's thick glass as it takes me beneath the ocean's surface.

My death ray has cleansed the world of aquatic life, but there's still plenty to see. I take in the sight of sunken ships, warplanes, and rusted spheres with huge spikes. The graveyard remnant of a war long ago spreads as far as I can see.

Minutes later, the lift slows then stops. I slide open the accordion barrier, a pair of outer hydraulic doors hiss and part, and I enter a cylindrical room with oval-shaped windows around the periphery, each framed by a copper-gold alloy with giant, stylized rivets. Various bots in the shapes of swordfish, beluga whales, sharks, octopus, and rays swim outside. Their visible pistons and gears turn and crank.

Inside, curving, waist-high shelves house objects both curious and wondrous, from hardcover books and graphic novels to screening discs, framed "postcards," carvings, pottery, and glassware, pilfered from cities that died long before my apocalyptic vision was a gleam in my eye. A model of Da Vinci's flying machine hangs from the ceiling alongside a fake sperm whale being attacked by a giant squid; a golden Egyptian sarcophagus and reclining Buddha lie next to a giant jade dragon; the assembled bones of a Tyrannosaurus Rex and a double-headed mammoth face each other as if to do battle.

Arranged to perfection, it's museum archives meets gentleman-collector-geomancy chic. I sometimes wander my elegant labyrinth of curiosities for hours—but not today.

On a shelf, between a singed, red hero's cowl with broken goggles and a shattered trident, a pair of simple, polished black marble supports beckon me.

"I've been waiting a long times for this," I say. I savor the moment as I lower the katana in its sheathe onto the cradles. It's exactly as satisfying as I always imagined—like putting the final piece of a puzzle into place. A part of me considers flashbacking so I can relive this instant, but I know better.

When one puzzle is done, it's time to start another.

"And so I shall."

I hum a few bars of opera and idly walk through the maze of trophies and treasures from my many exploits and expeditions. In passing, I admire a set of Fabergé eggs plundered from a castle overrun with mutated vermin, a golden statue of Ganesha plucked from a temple about to be engulfed in lava, and a polished medieval battle-ax taken from the hands of one of Jupitar Island's most feared "heroes."

So many memories, each deserving of a cataloged account. At last, I can turn my attention to this task.

I reach the center of my repository.

From a collection on a shelf, I remove a vinyl audio disk with grooves etched into its black surface and place it on a gramophone of polished wood with a brass horn. I wind its crank, lift its arm, and gently lower the needle at its tip onto the hypnotically spinning record. A tremulous opera fills the chamber with just a hint of crackle and pop from the antiquated technology.

The acoustics are perfection. If only the former denizens of this planet had stayed out of my way as I vied to make this world a better place, they might have gotten to enjoy the elegance of my genius. Ah well, sometimes one must start from scratch.

I hum along as I pass a sleek convertible with rounded detailing and cog-shaped etchings. In the driver's seat, a submariner in a rounded brass diver's helmet with breathing tubes attached to a canister on the passenger seat grips the wheel with thick leather gloves seamlessly attached to watertight coveralls made of leopard seal hide.

Normally, I would give him a little bow; it's our thing. Today,

I'm too excited. My heart thumps in my temples as I approach my gilded writing desk, which is made of giant gears, steam whistles, and gauges salvaged from a factory, all drenched in half-melted gold. The matching chair—more aptly called a throne—has a towering, imposing back and rounded arms softened by richly padded, dark red velour with button indents.

I reach the chair, lower myself onto its cushiony memory foam, and sigh as it perfectly accommodates my posterior. With a mere nudge of my pointing finger, I manipulate a joystick on the arm; in response, the chair glides on a track embedded into the glass floor and stops at a predetermined distance from the gleaming desk.

On the polished surface before me is an antique typewriter, a ream of crisp, white paper, and a Victorian telephone. I do love the opulent indulgences of the olden-olden days. I pick up the handset, press it to my ear, and dial zero. A bot on the other end bleeps at me.

"I'm not to be disturbed," I instruct.

The click as I hang up is wonderfully satisfying; there's just something about certain auditory textures.

I flourish my hand over the ream of paper, lift the top sheet with my thumb and pointing finger, align the page with the typing device, and roll the paper into place. Like a master pianist about to play the concerto of a lifetime, my fingers hover on the typewriter's rounded keys, which bear the glyphs of my personalized language.

Memoirs of a Time Master, I type. I depress the line-space carriage twice to leave a space under the title and continue—clack, clack, clack.

I shall begin at the end. After many tireless rewinds, I have saved the universe from the cruelty of life—by annihilating it. Ordinarily, I would posit that a fulsome examination of my motives is neither necessary nor productive, for what's done is done.

However, as this is a memoir, the whole point is to look back at the journey of a man's, woman's, or non-binary's life to reflect on those turning points that made him/her/zir who they are. Furthermore, as the title more than implies, I am capable of going back in time. Ergo, I could backflash and undo all of this. I shall not. My rationale for staying the course most certainly merits in-depth exploration and, indeed, forms the backbone of the treatise to follow.

The music of clattering keys becomes a symphony in my head, my fingers grow surer, and dare I say, they start to dance.

Fools might think I would come to regret my actions, that I have doomed myself to falling into a well of loneliness and boredom. These lesser beings fail to realize nothing is lonelier than being on the outside looking in at those who are together, nor does everyone share an obsessive need for socialization. I learned long ago the most-worthy company is my own and that of my creations. I now have the rest of my life to enjoy both.

My literary endeavor fills my belly with warmth.

I have so many thoughts to share with the only audience that matters—me!

In my youth, I had little patience for writing. Had I but known it was a form of puzzle making—finding the pieces and pattern for orderly assembly—a scribe I might have been!

For the next month, I do little else but indulge in the craft. I take breaks to reread but never revise—there is no need! I'm getting it all on the first take.

My post-apocalyptic life is turning out as wonderfully as I had planned—Twinkies, time to enjoy my collection, and days filled with well-earned self-congratulatory pontificating.

It's perfect—until *she* comes along.

Chapter 5

The day it all goes to muck starts like any other.

In the morning, the self-adjusting tint of the large clock window does its job, allowing entry to the perfect amount of light to ease me out of slumber. I yawn drowsily in a bejeweled egg-shaped bed embedded in a dais (we call it the nest) near the summit of my abode.

Genetrix helps me stand, zips me into a strongman-style striped unitard, and fastens a gleaming brace with rivets and cogged joints around my leg; they whir pleasantly as my daily ritual unfolds with such wonderful repetitive predictability, it's like the best parts of a timeloop without any of the dangers.

I stroll along a semi-circular ramp to a platform several measures below and admire a myriad of piston-and-pulley exercise devices of my own design. After a series of light physiotherapeutic movements, I traverse a bridge to an antiquated barber's chair where I lie back as Genetrix lasers my teeth, trims my goatee, and buffs my nails.

Under her watchful "eye," I pop a nutrient pill and wash it down with fizzy black soda pop drawn from a steam-pressured copper spout. Only then does she prepare a breakfast from my vast food stores, serving it to me at a grand dining table on delicate plates of blown glass. I munch delightedly on a repast of seared artificial bacon, potato chips, and mini cheese quiches.

Genetrix bleeps as other bots clear the table.

"Indeed," I agree, "it's time to dress."

She projects a hologram of various outfits and accessories.

"No, no, no," I chide, followed by, "Next!" as she shows me a feathered bicorn hat, silk ascots, and leather suspenders. None of them fit my mood until …

"Ah, yes, there!" I say.

Genetrix clucks in approval, and a clear conduit overhead spits a Victorian gentleman's ensemble into her waiting arms. She helps me out of my leg brace and into a pair of pantaloons then bleeps as she struggles to button a vest over my growing belly.

"*You* need to go on a diet," I snap. I pat my gut proudly. "This is a sign of success. You'll just have to get me new outfits from that boutique I like in Jupitar City. You know, the one with the top hats."

The robot chirps in response.

"Quite right," I chuckle. "They're never open, but now, they're also never closed."

Genetrix hands me a golden cane with a stylized spaceship for a handle. I could use a hoverchair, but I like to get in my steps. I take care descending a circular staircase—with my leg, its tricky, but I enjoy the challenge, and architecturally, the spirals are divine. I reach the base of the stairs and stride past bots wiping spotless surfaces with disinfectant towelettes.

"Inventory report?" I ask Genetrix as we walk toward my bird-cage elevator. "Begin with nourishment and water supplies."

The bot bleeps, bloops, and dings as we enter the lift.

"Excellent." I close the accordion door, spin the crank, and we descend amidst suspended platforms, sweeping ramps, and hanging oil paintings. "And the repurposing of construction drones from the reclamation colonies? Are we on schedule? I want to be ready to start my next project as soon as my manuscript is complete. The blueprints are exquisite."

The bot answers with a chirp as we whoosh below the ocean's crashing waves.

"Stupendous. And the oxygenators around the planet? What's their status? Some of us need to breathe, you know."

Genetrix replies with another affirmative bleep, projecting a hologram of maintenance bots tending to a global network of vented, tall, tubular shafts. Even before I swept all life from the planet, there weren't enough plants to keep the atmosphere breathable.

"All is in hand then."

The elevator stops. Genetrix gets the door for me.

"Thank you," I incline my head politely.

As she rolls out, her hand spins, opens, and sprouts a splay of feathers.

"Start over there," I point at my katana trophy.

She bleeps condescendingly.

"Yes, in fact, I do think you're my servant," I snort.

She shakes her head and starts dusting the trident *next* to the katana, intentionally defiant. I'd say I'm allowing her personality subroutines to remain as is to keep me humble, but that is of no interest.

"I'll see you at snack time," I say over my shoulder.

As she dusts, I leisurely follow a meandering route through my maze of treasures. Beyond the windows, a school of mechanical jellyfish bob and glow. When I reach the center of the labyrinth, I put a record of bittersweet melodies onto the gramophone and turn its cranks. A warbling tune echoes out of the horn.

If I were to throw a masquerade ball, I imagine this is what the live band would play. I bow deeply to the deep-sea diver at the wheel of the automobile.

"Would you care to dance?"

He replies with insightful silence.

"Well said," I answer. I take a moment to admire my reflection in the glass of his round porthole before I turn to gaze longingly at the antique typewriter on my golden desk of cogs and pistons. "My partner *is* waiting."

Smiling at my playfulness—*Funny* and *handsome*, I think—I lower my growing bottom onto the indented seat of my throne, press the joystick on the armrest that causes it to slide forward, and stop it a little further from my desk than I used to—to accommodate my growing girth.

Perhaps I should do a sit-up or two as part of my routine. I laugh immediately. *What am I, an athlete?*

"*Ridiculum.*" My head shakes with superiority, and I dab away a mirthful tear with a lace hanky.

I set it down, and my fingers tingle with anticipation as I place them on the anachronistic typing device. I stare at the blank sheet before me. This is it; this is the final page of my memoir. I would've completed it last night if I hadn't fallen asleep at the keys. I blubbered and curled inward as Genetrix gently rocked me in her arms, took me up the lift, and tucked me into the nest.

Now, awake and caffeinated from my soda beverage, I clack at the typewriter with the sure strokes of a literary genius.

Within an hour, my masterpiece is complete. Nearby, Genetrix feather dusts an already immaculate shelf displaying crowns and scepters of long-dead royalty. I barely notice. My gaze is fixated on the closing line. I clear my throat and read it aloud.

"This is *not* a new beginning for humanity," I shout. "This truly is their END."

Genetrix pauses in her work; her face pulses with pastel colors, and she bleeps encouragingly.

"Indeed," I agree.

I pull the sheet free of the typewriter and admire my closing words for a count of three. As satisfying as this is, there is one more moment that I've been imagining. Putting the last piece of any puzzle in its place is always—to quote the linguistically banal—the best.

I ready the page like a fighter pilot bringing a warplane in for a landing, about to place my craft atop the thick pile of paper that is my autobiography—except, I don't see it.

"But I always keep it on the right," I murmur. Yet, it isn't there!

I look to the left, back to the right, then behind my typewriter. I even look under it, to no avail. My manuscript—it's gone!

"Genetrix!" I shout. "I will *not* tolerate practical jokes!" I'm not fooling on that score. I'll strip her down to basic functions if it comes to it. "Where is my memoir?"

The bot makes three sad blipping noises; her face goes dark; her form flops limp; her arms and feather duster dangle.

"Genetrix?"

This isn't some drollery. She's powered down. I grab my telephone and dial zero. There's no tone. I click the hang-up button repeatedly to no avail. This isn't possible. The tech may look antiquated, but it's beyond top of the line.

"Robots!" I shout futilely into the device.

"Settle down," a womanly voice responds.

I squeal and fumble the receiver; it thuds onto the desk.

Grasping my chest, I turn to face the deep-sea diver, but it's not he who spoke. Standing next to the convertible, with her back to me, is a metallic pink robot with an hourglass figure wearing a blond wig that curls around her ears. I push myself to my feet and clumsily get behind my chair to use it as a shield. Is she one of my collectibles come to life? No, I'd remember her.

"Who ... What are you?" I ask.

"We call this model Mairī Lin," she coos with a voice that's seductively babyish.

We?

Her wavy blond hair bounces as she spins around with a ballerina's grace.

Her shiny visage has the general form of eyes, nose, mouth, and ears, all in shades of pink; they are more artistic interpretation than literal rendering, like a mannequin brought to life. Her "eyes" and "lips" make micro-movements as she speaks and reacts. There's a serpentine quality to the way she gestures her arms, twirls her wrists, and tilts her head—as if her joints were for show—creating a beguiling, inhuman effect.

I almost approve—automatons should move like automatons, otherwise what's the point?—until I see what the *rosea machina* holds in her shiny hands.

My eyes widen.

"My manuscript!" I wail.

She perches a pair of magnetic spectacles she can't possibly need on her tiny nose. A mechanical hammerhead swims by outside.

"You know, some people think that because I look the way I do," she gestures at her hyper-feminized form, still talking in a sexualized infantile tone, "that I don't like to read. It's not easy being a beautiful woman, but it's much harder to be an ugly one."

She flips through the manuscript.

"Put that down immediately!" I demand.

"Gladys, are you getting all this?" she asks, ignoring me.

"Gladys?" I demand. "Who's Gladys?" *And how did she survive my death ray?*

"Robots!" I shout toward the lift. Their custom sensors are sensitive enough to hear me in the base above (if barely), yet there's no response. I realize why. A black pod, the size of a fist, floats in the air a few measures away.

"A muffler," I grunt. It's impairing all outgoing communications from this room, electronic and vocal.

I grab my cane and lift it overhead, ready to smash the inhibitor that's preventing my loyal bots from hearing me. Once that's done, they'll blast this scrap-heap-walking to smithereens.

"I wouldn't," the pink intruder says.

"I would," I snort.

She points a pink laser pistol at me. I drop the cane; it thuds on a Persian carpet; my hands go up. Sweat beads my brow and drips into my eyes. I prefer to be brave when it's advantage me.

It is *advantage you*, I remind myself. *You're the time traveler.*

I raise a fair point. All I have to do to turn the tables on this wench is go back to last night, set a trap, and bam. Game, set, and match.

"Chapter 3," she enunciates with a babyish yet sexually charged breathiness. "The Rules of Time Travel."

"How are you reading my secret language?" I demand.

"Oh, you know," she shrugs mysteriously.

"No, I do not know!" I stamp my foot. "Tell me."

She doesn't elaborate. When I get my hands on her, I'll pull the answer from her drive, overwrite her OS, and rewire her voice box. Robots should sound like robots. That's part of their charm, divesting them of bothersome inflections that, along with facial expressions and body language, form a near-indecipherable set of social cues that everyone who is not me manages to read as naturally as they breathe.

Dear society, you want to use non-verbal communication? Try Morse code! At least then everyone's on an equal footing.

I reach for the internal switch in my brain that will undo this miserable interaction by vaulting my present psyche into my past self, allowing me to set a trap for this interloper.

"Rule number one," she continues.

I pause. If I go back in time, I'll lose some of what I've written, which is wholly unacceptable. I'm in charge here, and I will *not* compromise a single page, a single word, a single punctuation mark for this invader!

"Not even a typo," I whisper as I spot an eviscerator pistol strapped to the inside of my desk. I put it there several jumps back ago to shoot the protector with the katana in the back, but after a Butterfly Effect, I haven't needed it for some timelines now.

"You don't mind if I sit, do you?" I ask, grasping the brace around my leg and wincing.

The feminized automaton gestures her pistol permissively toward my velour throne. I sit. She lounges against the convertible like she's posing for the cover of a magazine.

"I can only travel back through my own existence, into a younger version of myself," she continues. With her caricaturized voice, she makes it sound like she's reading erotica.

Is she making fun of me? Without my social-ometer, I haven't a clue. Would my lie detector even work on her?

My fingers close about the handle of the eviscerator; it's cool to my touch. I could blast her right through the desk. I start squeezing the trigger, then hesitate. No one's read my work before, not even Genetrix, but when she does, I've triple-checked her algorithms to make sure she doesn't utter a single criticism and shares effusive praise.

But this *rosea machina*, I have no control over her code. I stare into her robot eyes the way I hated to with a living person.

I'm caught between fear that this AI will despise what I've written and the hope that she'll love it. The former makes me want to blast her; the latter, to spare her—temporarily. I lean forward, waiting for her to continue.

"Beware of repeating perfect moments," she reads.

She holds my memoir aside and looks at me.

"Really?" she asks.

The design of her form has some aesthetic merits, and despite my understandable fascination with my own text, my mind drifts as I follow the curves of her hips and breasts. I shake my head to snap my reverie.

"That's what I wrote," I say.

"Well, this is disappointing," she sighs.

"No, it isn't!" I declare defensively. How dare she criticize my work?!

"I had a whole business plan for a time-traveling cruise ship so folks could relive their happiest memories. They'd be tourists in their own life."

My eyes widen in alarm. "A time ship?"

"Powered by a wormhole drive, obviously!" she giggles.

My grip tightens on the concealed eviscerator. Time travel's *my* thing.

"Oh, don't worry," she waves her free hand at me, laughing at my clear concern. "My temporal tinkering was purely theoretical. The schematics were in crayon. I was six."

My breathing eases, and my brow raises with piqued interest. "Schematics, you say."

If Genetrix were online, she'd rightly chide me. I need to focus on the matter at hand. From the sounds of things, this AI has been embedded with memories—real or otherwise—or this Gladys person is speaking through the pink robot. I need to trace the transmission back to the source so I can end her and co-opt this technology for myself. I'm already getting redesign ideas for my robot army.

"My quantum vessel was going to be utter luxury," the pink machine continues, oblivious to the minutes of her existence counting down. "There would be discount fares, of course, equity and all that, and a gift shop. So many merchandising opportunities, and the tag lines!"

"*Nunc futuri*," I declare before I can stop myself, twirling my free hand grandly overhead. She keeps pulling me in!

"Future now," she translates.

My fingers relax around the trigger of the eviscerator as I await her praise for my most wondrous of catchphrases.

"I was thinking more like, Yesterday Today, you know?" she says. "It's more accessible. Has a cozy, family feel."

My grip tightens. "It's terrible."

"The whole idea's terrible according to this," she flops my manuscript up and down.

"Careful with that!"

She raises a finger to silence me—the audacity!—and returns to my book. I should shoot her right now, but I know she'll love this next part. I may be a villain, but I'm not a monster. I will grant her the joy of my prose before I end her.

"Repeating a favorite instance will result in one of three undesirable ends," she reads. To my surprise, she drops the sexy baby persona, and her delivery becomes not wholly terrible.

"First, while striving to relive a golden moment, I may inadvertently do something differently, spoiling the course of not only that event, but others to come. This type of error creates a near irresistible urge to go back again to make a course correction. My statistical analysis confirms that these types of do-overs are high risk with negative yields. *Ipso facto*, the more I strive to make things right, the more likely I am to make everything go wrong."

"It's utterly frustrating," I murmur.

"Do you suppose it has anything to do with the atomic vibrations associated with such pivotal, emotional junctures?" She shrugs prettily and tosses her hair. "But what do I know? I'm just a ditz!"

I should be asking her again about Gladys, yet when she uses terms like "atomic vibrations," I find it hard to breathe. I wonder if the pink automaton's hair is silky soft or has a synthetic plastic feel. Does she style it? Would she like me to comb it?

"Danger number two," she reads, tapping her chin with her pistol. "I journey to relive a favorite moment, and I get it right, repeating everything exactly the same as before. There can be a thrill to being the only person who knows what's about to happen; sadly, this is frequently *not* the case for the most special of memories. In these instances, it is often the unknown and the unexpected that make a moment what it is. I loathe spontaneity, but without it, I'm pained to say, some of the shiniest intertwining of events are dulled by predictability."

The *rosea machina* begins pacing back and forth, reading more passionately, sounding even less like a bimbo nympho caricature and more like a candidate for the position of First Minister.

"If these two examples fail to convince that trying to repeat happy recollections is doomed to taint the very memories one is hoping to recapture, I offer the third, and most dangerous, potential outcome of this fool's errand—success."

I sit up straighter. This is the most important rule of them all.

"You have read correctly," she recites. "On one occasion, when I backflashed to relive a glorious moment, I got every detail right, and it was just as sublime as I remembered—so I did the only logical thing; I went back to live it again. Part of me did worry that experiencing it a third time would lack the luster of rounds one and two. How wrong I was. If anything, the sensations intensified. I rewound again, and again, and again. Each time was more magnificent than the one before. It was like the most addictive of drugs—one that becomes more potent, not less, with every use. I craved more. To quote the less evolved, I fed the beast.

"Before I knew it, I'd trapped myself in a loop of perfection. Some have imagined the mythological notion of hell to be a nightmare moment repeated over and over. If so, then this was the opposite; it was heaven, and I was ecstatic to be there, forever—until I felt something start to give.

"It began as a thin, intermittent whine. Then I noticed some of the colors were off, either faded or too bright with white light. Strips of blackness would appear and disappear. It was as if I were wearing the moment thin like an overplayed videocassette from days gone by. Time can bend, but can it also snap? If so, what might that do to me?

"Like the memory itself, I could feel myself tearing apart. Worse, the very centrifugal temporal forces that were killing me did not want to release me. They pulled me in tighter.

"By sheer will, I escaped, if barely, and not unscathed. To this day, I'm haunted by an insatiable desire to rewind to the one memory I dare never revisit."

My spine tingles, and my whole body tightens at her words —*my* words. Weakness wells in my eyes. I wipe them dry.

The pink robot looks up from the pages and pushes back her

blond hair. "I wonder what memory would be so tantalizing for a man like you that you'd never want to leave it?"

"The one where I kill you," I reply.

I fire the eviscerator. The green beam blasts through the desk and cuts off a lock of her hair. I duck as the beam flies past Genetrix's inert form, bounces off the gramophone's shiny horn, and buzzes through the air where my head was a moment ago. The green streak of energy burns through the velour chair, hits the golden Egyptian sarcophagus, and ricochets off a series of other polished items.

"You are a terrible shot," she says as she twists out of the way of the bouncing beam.

"Am I?" I reply.

The green energy hits the sonic dampener, slicing it in half. The pieces clatter onto the edge of my desk and bounce to the floor.

I grab the phone's receiver, dial zero, and shout, "Intruder alert!"

"I wanted to play some more," she pouts, "but I guess I'll have to skip to killing you."

She aims her weapon. My eyes widen. I reach for my internal time switch. I *really* don't want to rewrite a single word of my manuscript; I also don't want to die.

A dozen of my robots drop down the glass shaft connecting my library to the base above and fly over the shelves of my labyrinth. They hover and squawk angrily, unleashing a volley of bullets and beams that pierce and melt the intruder's pink form. She dances spastically as she's hit again and again, releasing blue goo from within her shell. My manuscript flies from her hands; pages flutter everywhere.

"Do *not* hit my book!" I order.

The intruder falls; pages drift and settle around her. What's left of her battered and charred body twitches and sparks in a pool of her blue blood. I stride to her severed head and hold it above me in Shakespearean style.

"Where be your gibes now?" I demand.

The pink entity's ocular orifices pulse unexpectedly; her skull whines as something within powers up, vibrating her disheveled hair. I shriek, drop the head, and hop back. As an evil mastermind, I know that sound all too well.

"It's an auto-destruct!" I cry.

My robots form a protective circle around me.

"Round ... one ... goes to you ... my Timematician," the pink head struggles to say.

"That's not my name!" I insist—even if the moniker has a certain ring to it.

A puff of smoke blows out her ear; the whining dissipates, and her eyes flicker. I wait for three heartbeats, but her auto-destruct fails to activate. It must've been damaged when my bots shot her to pieces.

She sighs robotically, and as her eyes go dark, she says, "See you ... soon."

Chapter 6

I stare at the decapitated head. Where did the robot come from? How did it get past my defenses? Who is its creator? Is it Gladys? And …

"What did she mean, see you soon?" I ask aloud.

My robots shrug in unison and bleep that there's "insufficient data."

"Useless!" I shout.

I lean on my cane, walk to Genetrix, and slap her on the back; she bloops, straightens, and looks about in confusion. I point at the pink metal head. "Take it to my laboratory!"

Genetrix obeys as the other robots collect the pages of my manuscript. I recall the pink entity reading it out loud.

Did she like it? I wonder. I shake my head at my own ridiculousness. *Of course, she did!* Not that I care.

Thankfully, Genetrix missed it all so I don't have to deal with her scolding me for letting myself get so distracted.

A bot brings me an impenetrable treasure chest stylized with decorative cogs, polished metal handles, and a compass in the center.

"*Patentibus*," I cry. It releases a hiss of air, and the lid pops back. Within is a single key with an ornate spider and web for a head. I remove it, lower my manuscript into the padded interior, and place the key on top.

"*Arcanus!*" I command. The lid dutifully pops shut.

I wave the bot away.

"Triple my security protocols!" I bark as I take the head from Genetrix, tuck it under my arm, and stride into the oversized birdcage.

It sweeps me up, clangs to a halt, and when I shove the accordion doors open, I forget about getting my steps in. I activate the hover tech embedded in my belt and fly past winding staircases and arching ramps. I land on a platform with a marble work slab. On it sit a slew of antique-looking, hyper-stylized laser pens, saws, baby mallets, drills, and probes. Next to them, a prototype charcoal skin-suit made of a rubberized polymer looks like an abandoned flesh sack from a horror film. Adding to the monster-movie motif, a pair of huge electrodes crackle behind me.

I shove the deflated golem-esque work-in-progress to the side, set the pink head on the slab, and Genetrix helps me into a white lab coat. She squawks about the importance of tidiness (as if I didn't program that into her) and neatly folds the polymer skin.

Ignoring her, I fasten the leather straps of my work goggles behind my head and fire up a laser scalpel. With all of my grand plans, I hardly have time for this; yet how can I proceed without first eliminating this one remaining threat? Besides, who can resist a good post-mortem?

Quickly and proficiently, I slice the ligaments fastening the blond wig to the pink cranium, pry open the head plating, and locate her detonation device. It's the size and shape of what was once known as a triple-A battery. I confirm that my bots indeed damaged the self-destruct mechanism in their assault, preventing it from operating to spec, but I'm not taking any chances. I remove it from its protective casing with a pair of tongs and place it on a circular plate. Genetrix lowers a glowing glass bell over it and fastens a round, copper gauge to the clear dome.

She hands me a square remote with a single button. I press it, the device emits an activation wave, and without a protective casing, the exposed explosive erupts. The needle on the gauge flies all the way into the red as the concussive output goes off the charts, cracking the glass.

"*Deodamnatus!*" I swear in surprise. Genetrix gasps in agreement.

My sensors are easily capable of reading the energetic output of all existing explosive weaponry so either my equipment is malfunctioning—or this is something new.

I wipe my brow with the sleeve of my lab coat.

"Genetrix," I bark, "run a diagnostic."

As she does, I look more closely at the pink head's innards. It's a bizarre combination of siliconic and biotech, unlike anything I've seen. Whoever built this thing was a genius. Perhaps, dare I say it, a peer?

"Gladys," I murmur. Is that a codename? An acronym? Who, or more likely, what, is she?

Finding out has become my top priority. Surely my death ray killed the pink obscenity's creator, though not his/her/zirs inorganic construct.

*Construct*s, plural, I correct myself.

The *rosea machina* is safely dismantled, but her G.L.A.D.-S counterpart is still out there.

"Just my luck," I mutter. I hand my drill to Genetrix and pull off my silicone gloves. "I finally destroy humanity, and someone's left this mess for me to clean up."

The robot bleeps as she puts the drill into its place in a vacuum-sealed drawer alongside a bevy of other tools and slides it shut.

"Yes, I know she spoke as though there were more of her out there; that's what I'm saying, if you ever bothered to listen." I raise a finger imperiously in the air. "But this won't be a problem for long."

I walk up a ramp to my *dominus imperium*. I press buttons, turn dials, and check monitors. A hologram of the planet forms before me.

"Peek a boo, I see you," I say as a red light flashes, representing one of the many municipalities abandoned during the wars between dregs and Supergenics. My brow furrows.

That can't be right.

"On screen," I order.

My monitors fill with images of different colored feminized robots and construction drones working amidst decaying skyscrapers. Water sparkles in the bay behind them, along with a massive bridge. A pink twin of the decapitated bot on my workbench turns toward my spy cam. She waves as if she can see me, winks, snaps her finger, and the images of her and the city fizzle out.

The blood drains from my face. My body trembles. Genetrix bleeps at me. My head swivels toward the bot.

"Do *not* tell me to stay calm." I point at the screen. "*That* is *my* city, and I won't let that pink abomination have it. Robots! Prepare for battle!"

WITHIN THE HOUR, I fly over a massive bridge and touch down in my battle armor outside the crumbling metropolis my pesky mechanical opponent has overtaken. Behind me, a bay ripples with pristine blue waters littered with dilapidated docks, rusty cranes, and semi-sunk cargo ships. A crescent-shaped mountain range capped with snowy peaks frames the other three sides of the urban center.

Genetrix lands next to me, along with thousands of my armed bots.

I gaze in disgust at an armada of feminized automatons and colorful AI construction vehicles flying about towers of glass, steel, and concrete on the verge of collapse.

A part of me notes that the drones are carefully positioning metal beams to bolster the buildings my feasibility surveys had deemed salvageable. Similarly, the crew of colorful bots is demolishing the edifices my recon units had classified as beyond repair. I consider allowing these interlopers to proceed. They seem capable enough to do the drudge work. I can oust and eradicate the *rosea machina*—and her hive—once the shoring, mooring, and, let's be frank, boring phase is complete.

She may mock me, foolishly believing I've turned tail to run, but the last laugh is always mine. So I think until a machine on caterpillar treads rumbles out of a trench. Atop the vehicle, a mechanical arm lifts and aims a giant bore toward the ground.

"What is—"

The drill buzzes and whines, spinning a massive cone ridged with serrated burrs that burrows into cracked concrete. The bore retracts and other construction machines ram and pound giant pylons into the exposed earth, providing foundations for fanciful facades that drones speedily weld into place.

Now *that* I cannot allow.

"Stop this at once!" I shout.

A pink robot with an hourglass figure—the twin to the one I destroyed in the library—waves at me. "There you are!" Her voice is as seductively babyish as her previous incarnation. She wears a neon pink safety vest she can't possibly need; blond hair pokes out from a matching hardhat.

Genetrix assesses the attire, which has a strange erotic appeal, and bleeps in a judgmental way.

"I don't care how she's dressed," I insist. "Just be quiet."

I stomp forward; the tread of my massive boots cracks concrete and leaves a trail of imposing footprints behind me. I stop before her, my form towering above hers.

"What do you think you're doing?" I demand. "This is *my* city."

Her pink pseudo-eyes blink with exaggerated slowness. "*Your* city? Your name's not on it. I did check."

"My name's on everything!" I shout back.

"Well, that's just greedy," she snips, turning her back on me.

Genetrix growls.

"Hush," I tell her, though my lead bot does raise a fair point. I *could* simply destroy the rose-colored interloper. I am Doctor BetterThan, which includes being better than her. But I don't like it when Genetrix starts pushing me around. Doing what she says will simply reinforce those irritatingly bossy subroutines like a most-listened-to playlist. Besides, there's something satisfying about making a lesser being like this blond bot recognize my superiority through intellectual rather than physical force.

"Look here," I say. My goggles project a holographic display of the plans I've devised for remaking the defunct municipality. Monorails run through Art Deco towers; steam, windmills, and hydro dams power clock towers, street lamps, and clicking inter-locking cogs; public squares house fountains with statues of me in the center.

I wait for her to concede the genius of my vision. She tilts her head, no doubt trying to take it all in.

"Cute," she says.

"Cute?" I demand. "It's magnificent."

"It has a certain charm," she concedes.

I incline my head. "I graciously accept your surrender." I don't mention that I will, of course, have to wipe her operating system and replace it with my own. AIs can be so touchy. "If you'd kindly step aside, I can proceed with my design."

"But," she says, "mine's better." Her eyes glow, my holo plans sputter, and my architectural rendering is replaced by a bastardized version of itself.

Holographic gondolas and funiculars obliterate my monorail; phallic constructs of polished metal rear through, shatter, and replace my Deco edifices; giant crystal orchids overgrow parkettes that should be filled with statues paying homage to my genius.

"I have soooo many ideas!" she says.

I shake with rage. "You stole my plans and perverted them!"

My voice modulator transforms my sputtering into a bellow.

She giggles and twirls her hair. "*I* stole *your* plans? My dear Timematician—"

"That's *not* my name," I snap. "I'm Doctor BetterThan."

"Are you, though?" she asks through her near-motionless lips. "We both know your blueprints are modified from the ones *you* stole from Empress Evangelikal."

"How do you …" I stop myself from saying any more.

"That's all you are," she continues. "A time thief. Your robots were designed by Judge Dreadnought, your suit by The Man, and your death ray on the moon, the one you're *so* proud of, well, that's *my* design, you shameless little pirate."

My look of shock is hidden within my helm.

"You're—"

"Mairī Lin Monroe," she coos. "The one, the only, is now the many."

Her reputation precedes her, but I always thought it hyperbole.

"Timematician," she says, "can I call you Tim for short?"

"You may not!" I snap.

Genetrix bleeps at Mairī Lin insultingly.

"Well, she's rude," Mairī Lin says.

"You're rude." I tap my goggles, and the city hologram warbles out.

"I *am* being rude," she agrees. "Introductions are in order. Meet my lady-matons." She tilts her head as three similar but different versions of herself land next to her.

"This is Gladys," Mairī Lin says of a shorter, petite green simulacrum with the shape of spectacles around her eyes. Her dark green hair looks molded to her head in perfect swoops.

"G.L.A.D.-S," I murmur. "Glib Android Despot. Model S."

"You gave her an acronym," Mairī Lin giggles. "You are adorable!

"My name is an homage to Dr. Gladys West," the green one tsks at me.

"She's our analytical alter," Mairī Lin says. "The brains of the operation. Saraswati," she gestures at a four-armed orange version of herself with a splay of freckles over the bridge of her nose and a red mohawk, "is our artistic self. The orchids were her idea."

Genetrix mutters.

Yes, I agree. *I will dismember this Saraswati first.*

A tall, muscular, broad-shouldered, purple version of the other three brightly hued robots stands like a hunting panther.

"And Dahomey is our protector," Mairī Lin says. "She named herself in honor of the Amazonians of Africa, the warrior women of what was once known as Black Sparta, from the before days."

"I know what Dahomey means," I lie. How dare she make me feel ill-informed?!

Dahomey's scalp is as bare and shiny as the rest of her. The perma-glare etched into her face, the oversized pistol magnetically stuck to one hip, and the metal cylinder clinging to the other make me swallow reflexively.

Mairī Lin introduces these three as if they were individuals, but behind them are a dozen more of each purple, green, and orange model. Do they prefer singular or plural pronouns? Does it vary by how many are present? Would I appear ignorant if I asked?

"And now you've met my whole system," Mairī Lin says. "I'm the primary. The queen bee, if you will, although royalty is based on barbaric feudal history that is frankly gross, and we don't follow an insect hive structure either. We're a pack collective."

In unison, the multitude of lady-matons, those before me and the ones directing construction bots in the busted city, turns to me. In a chorus, they say, "The one is many, and the many are one."

It's eerie, robotic, and for that ephemeral moment, rather wonderful—then they go back to acting like individuals. Inundated by a bevy of emotions, I momentarily forget about the city and my plans for rebuilding it and this world.

"I'm impressed," I admit—and infuriated. Am I also intimidated? Could this truly be *the* Mairī Lin Monroe—or at least a cybernetic representation of her split into these cybernetic bodies? It seems impossible. Yet, if anyone could pull off a psyche transfer from a biological body into mechanized ones—plural—it's her.

I must take a closer look at that pink head of hers back in my laboratory—a *very* close look, for she was absolutely correct when she labeled me a tech thief. And I've never seen any tech as transformative as this. I can't wait to make it my own—assuming any of what she says is true. Villains—techniacs in particular—are prone to hyperbole.

Either way, I can't resist imagining what it would be like to transfer my psyche into a robot form. I would no longer need my armor suits, for I would *be* the armored suit! Would that mean giving up my power, which is tied to my biological form? Even Mairī Lin has failed to create time travel tech. Do I care? Wasn't my goal to create a world in which do-overs were unnecessary?

And what about Twinkies? Robots have no need of such sustenance, but I'm sure I could create a heightened reality subroutine to mimic the taste experience without the disgusting excremental consequences of consuming actual food. Yet, as Genetrix likes to remind me, if it sounds too good to be true …

"The last I heard," I challenge, "Mairī Lin Monroe was locked in the deepest hole The Asylum could dig after her failed cybernetic coup."

"My dear Timematician—"

"That's not my name."

"Are you a fan or just another creeper?"

"Neither," I reply—though I do admire her tech. Does that make me a fan?

She giggles. "You're funny."

"I am," I agree, "but I wasn't joking. You were summarily defeated and incarcerated for crimes against humanity—as if *that's* not an oxymoron. Yet you somehow transferred your psyche into these femme bots—"

"Lady-matons," she corrects.

She does have a knack for nomenclature. Should I start calling myself the Timematician? No, my time travel days are in the past, and there's so much more to me than my power.

"Yes, my uprising did not end well for me," Mairī Lin concedes with a sigh. "But, thanks to your death ray—"

"So now it *is* my death ray?" I ask.

"You stole it fair and square," Mairī Lin shrugs.

Dahomey bristles.

"And," Mairī Lin gives her warrior alter a simmer-down gesture before turning back to me, "you put it to good use."

"Not good enough," I snort, "*if* what you say is true. You claim to be Mairī Lin Monroe, but you could simply be an advanced AI."

"Oh, I'm all real," she assures me in a sultry tone.

"You expect me to believe that from a tech-barren cell, you were able to accomplish the most scientifically advanced feat ever in the history of this planet?"

"Analyzing vocal patterns," Gladys says robotically as if she's using her own version of a social-ometer. Did I steal that from her as well? Surely it won't work on me, not while I'm speaking through my vocal modifier.

"Transmitting analysis," Gladys says.

"Analysis received," Mairī Lin coos as if she were at the climax of a love scene. "You believe me—at least you want to."

Genetrix squawks at me.

Mairī Lin giggles. "Is she always so … motherly?"

"Quiet!" I mutter at my lead bot. "You're embarrassing me." To Mairī Lin, I say, "How did you do it?"

I try to sound imperious and demanding, but clearly my vocal filters can't hide my awe as I gesture at the rainbow quartet. I'm already envisioning what my robot bodies will look like once I make this tech my own. Hopefully, she's like most villains—so eager to brag they practically hand me their inventions.

"How indeed," Mairī Lin giggles. "That question *must* be killing you. I mean, there I was, my biological form strapped down in the most secure anti-technology cell in all of Jupitar Island, barely able to blink; I couldn't have been more helpless."

So one might suppose, yet I realize, what could be more dangerous than a genius with nothing to do but think? All she would need was one fool to give her an opportunity to act. I grasp the scattered pieces of this puzzle and quickly assemble them.

"The protector with the katana sought you out in your cell," I realize. My nemesis' final, taunting words flash through my mind. "She paid you a visit and asked for your advice on how to defeat me."

I can envision it so clearly—Caitlin Feral would stoop to any low to bring me down; she'd even turn to another villain.

"It was straight out of a screening!" Mairī Lin coos.

"Only a technius can stop a technius," I say, putting the clichéd pieces together.

"She was absolutely desperate! But why would I, a prisoner, help her?" Mairī Lin asks. "You *must* be wondering."

"Hardly," I reply. "By assisting my foe, you were hoping to create an opportunity for your escape."

She shrugs mischievously. "They took every precaution, but—"

"You're a genius," I finish for her. "And they were idiots."

"You know, the protector didn't believe me when I told her you were a time traveler—not at first. But she had just enough inherent chrono-sensitivity to have the uncomfortable sense that I *might* be right. I helped her train her brain so she could remember for herself —not everything, but enough. Ah, glorious déjà vu."

Caitlin said as much. I finally beat her, yet still she finds a way to haunt me. I'm tempted to rewind to make sure she never picks up a katana—but of course, I've already tried that. I shudder at how those timelines turned out.

Mairī Lin's near motionless lips manage a cartoonish smirk. Reading her expressions is definitely easier than the nuances of a biological person.

"Aren't you going to ask me how *I* knew you were at the nexus of all these time shifts?" she presses.

If she thinks she's baiting me, she's about to discover that I am the epitome of the gentleman hunter—sophisticated, armed, and deadly.

"I prefer to answer rather than ask," I snip. "You have an unusually strong sense of quantum disruptions, an aspect of your superhuman mind, no doubt. Every time I backflashed, it set off ripples, granting you visions of your own life in the futures in which I'd rewound. You knew, on some Supergenic level, these were memories of a sort. Being a scientist, you sought a scientific explanation. In time—"

"Times," she corrects.

I incline my head, acknowledging her correct usage of the plural form.

"In *times*, you narrowed it down to me."

"Gold star," she winks and slow claps. The first of the two gestures is crass; the latter is something I've been meaning to give a try.

"You should save your applause until the end," I say. Despite myself, my tone has a hint of playfulness within the rebuke.

Genetrix notices, bleeping at me questioningly. I ignore her.

"Once katana woman—"

"Caitlin," Mairī Lin says.

They're on a first-name basis?

"Once she believed you," I continue, "she asked you how to stop me. You devised quantum stabilizers and built them into the protector's throwing stars to keep me from time jumping."

"That was me," Gladys interjects.

"The bird shape was my idea," Saraswati adds.

"I made sure the weaponry remained balanced," Dahomey concludes.

"Silly bees," Mairī Lin says. "At the time, they," she points at the other lady-matons, "were all still integrated inside of my biological brain as a single persona."

"You/they," I say—experimenting with multi-personae language; now it's Gladys who inclines her head appreciatively— "were trapped in The Asylum, but as part of your design for the quantum stabilizers, you embedded hidden tech for your own agenda."

"You're right," Mairī Lin concedes. "I should've saved my slow clap until the end."

"Once the stars interfaced with my computer system, you had an escape hatch out of your body trapped in a cell. You hopscotched your data-encoded psyche through my optic network—"

"Then up into the satellite system," she points to the sky. "I bounced around a bit."

"Then you streamed into the dormant relay system of some secret, undiscovered backup lab of yours."

"Several unused prototypes were collecting dust," she says.

"Naturally," I agree. I have several such hideaways with stolen tech I've yet to master. Who doesn't?

Saraswati puts one of her four hands on the other bots and one on her breast. "We were positively dying for a download."

"And now here you are," I say.

Mairī Lin gives a demure curtsy. Genetrix's blank face lights up, about to say something.

"Shush," I silence her. She mutters just loud enough to hear.

"She really is annoying," Mairī Lin says.

"You don't even know," I agree with a chortle. "But Genetrix raises a fair point. According to your trial, you tried to move your consciousness into a robot once before, but it didn't take. That's why your coup failed, and you were captured."

"Perhaps it's true what they say," she sighs. "Ultimately, a techniac is always brought low by the failings of his/her/zirs own devices."

I think about how many of my do-overs have blown up in my face and nod knowingly.

"The cybernetic circuits kept shorting," Mairī Lin continues. "But alone in my cell, I had nothing but time to figure out where I went wrong and how to get it right."

As I hypothesized, I want to say.

"I was trying to download the entirety of my genius brain into a single framework," she elaborates like so many genius fools before her, giving away their secrets. "It couldn't handle the vastness of my intellect."

I look at her rainbow array of alters with greater appreciation. "You divided your psyche into distinct personas while maintaining a unifying core."

"The solution was so obvious; I can't believe it didn't occur to me before. Split, transfer, grow. Now, here we are." She laughs gaily and places her fingertips on my chest plating. I brush her hand away.

She shrugs. "Thank you for helping me free myself."

Whatever momentary appreciation and sense of kinship I may have had for her turns to sludge, and my breakfast Twinkie comes up my throat. I survey her armada of inorganic lady-matons. I lose count of the multiple duplicates of Gladyses, Saras, and Dahomeys amidst the construction drones. There is only the one pink bot— the primary—though I'm sure Mairī Lin has more backups waiting to be activated if this one fails.

While one Gladys, Saras, and Dahomey set is here with me, their duplicates continue the demolition and buttressing work. I watch green, orange, and purple lady-matons helping to rebuild the city—*my* city—and it's my own fault. Caitlin went to Mairī Lin because of me, giving her the opportunity to use me to free herself. I wait for Genetrix's recriminations, but in this instance, I have plenty of my own.

The Timematician—brought low by the failings of his own time travel.

69

Perhaps that should be the title of my autobiography.

My audio amplifiers let me hear the Gladyses directing the construction vehicles while the four-armed Saras interject with critiques on craftsmanship.

"What are you doing?" a Saras demands of a Gladys. "That support beam is going to completely ruin the sightline!"

"That support beam is going to keep the whole overpass from collapsing," the Gladys replies.

"We talked about this!" the Saraswati shouts.

"*You* talked about it," the Gladys responds. "I don't have time for your artsy-fartsy nonsense."

"That's it!" the Saraswati yells.

They look ready to fistfight when a towering purple Dahomey pushes them apart.

"If you two don't resolve this, I'm going to turn this bridge into a missile silo," the Dahomey threatens. Her perma-glare grows angrier.

"No!" the Saraswati says with horror. "That would ruin the whole motif!"

"And the structural reinforcements we would need for that," the Gladys groans, "we'd have to dig up and relay the whole foundation!"

All the Dahomeys turn and yell at them in unison, "Then figure it out!"

"I suppose I could use an arching system," the Gladys suggests.

"If it were patterned with roses, it wouldn't be so bad," the Saraswati concedes.

With that, they get back to work.

My heart throbs in my throat.

Reality is starting to overshadow the excitement I felt at the possibilities Mairī Lin's psyche-transfer tech opens up.

I came here believing these artificial creatures were mere left-overs from a mad genius killed by my/her/our death ray. But I now accept that these so-called "lady-matons" *are* the mad genius—and their forces are legion.

Not only that, but she's once bypassed my security systems to infiltrate my lair and has done the same with my projection goggles. Mairī Lin as she is now is too dangerous for me to face.

I have no choice. I have to go back in time to kill Mairī Lin Monroe before she can transfer her psyche from her biological body into these mechanical creatures. But, after I destroy her in the past, can I make this future happen again, or will I screw it up? Once she's dead, can I find her secret base and master her psyche transfer tech without learning more from her about how it works? And what about my memoirs? I groan at the thought of having to rewrite them from scratch. All that typing!

"You're ruining everything!" I shout at the pink lady-maton.

My jet pack surges to life, propelling me as I bionic punch her across the jaw. She smashes through a brick wall and disappears from view. Her army of builders stop and turn; blasters and missile launchers pop out from hidden compartments, all aimed at me. My bots assume battle formation. The Dahomeys arm themselves, pistols in one hand, blazing laser sabers in the other; that includes the Dahomey in front of me.

My armor activates a glowing protective energy shield, and a series of sonic booms tear the air as my armada of warplanes arrives.

The battle carriers land, and caterpillar tanks roll out. Rotating gears spin giant drills on their fronts and flail metal tentacles off their sides.

"Prepare for battle!" a Dahomey cries.

"Wait!" Mairī Lin shouts.

Everyone freezes as the pink automaton tosses her hardhat aside, primly wipes gravel off her shoulder, and adjusts her safety vest like its haute couture; her face isn't even dented.

"Are you sure this is what your wounded ego needs?" she asks, sashaying forward with the grace and sensuality of a model on a runway.

"Get out of my city!" I reply.

"Sometimes you just have to throw on a crown and remind them who they're dealing with," she sighs. She sounds as if she's quoting some great sage. She nods at Dahomey. "Over to you."

"Attack!" Dahomey jumps forward, firing her pistol and swinging a laser saber. A horde of armed workers and construction drones surge behind her.

I shout to my army, "Destroy them all!"

Chapter 7

My robots' cogs churn, and their pistons pump; her lady-matons' limbs move like snakes. The two sides surge together, pulverizing each other in a flurry of photon blasts and hand-to-hand combat. Genetrix goes fist to fist with a Dahomey and a Saras and tears them limb from multi-limb while unfurling a slew of psychologically curdling insights against our foe(s).

As the battle unfolds, the pink primary of this sisterly system sidles up to me. My armor assumes a karate battle-stance, ready to defend and strike, but she makes no move to assault me.

She cocks her head. "What's it like, being a time traveler?"

I blink within my helm. No one's ever asked me that—how could they?

"You read my memoirs," I say. "The answers are all there."

"I loved every word," she says.

"You did?" I ask suspiciously. My social-ometer is useless with her. Is she being sarcastic? Genuine?

"Your writing's tight *and* lyrical," she continues as the battle rages around us.

"Thank you?" My words come out a question; I don't know how to respond. That's how long it's been since anyone other than Genetrix has given me a hint of acknowledgment for my skill, and when my bot does, I sometimes feel like a dog she's trying to train through positive reinforcement, hoping to get me to consistently do what I'm told as I'm told.

"But I can't shake this sense that you're leaving something out," Mairī Lin presses as a missile explodes to our left. "What's it *like*?"

Most people toss words about like feathers; hers have weight. I place them on my mental scale.

"It's … complicated," I say.

"I imagine so," she replies.

One of my battle tank's lashing tentacles grab numerous lady-matons and smash them on the ground; blue goo sprays everywhere.

"Come," she says as the fighting intensifies. "I want to show you something."

I hesitate. I'm not the naive, socially awkward fool who once took the words of cruel classmates, a manipulative Mother, and backstabbing fellow villains to be literal truth. From sarcasm to outright lies, I have learned my lesson.

I will not follow this metallic monstrosity anywhere. So I believe, until …

"What's that sound?" I murmur. "Is that … music?"

Mairī Lin shrugs mysteriously, her quasi-lips smirking.

My audio amplifiers are definitely picking up a faint melody weaving amidst the carnage.

"Filter and amplify," I order.

Within moments, the aria plays at perfect volume within my helmet. Tears shimmer in my eyes, and now Mairī Lin and I smile together. I recognize the song. How could I not?

"*Amor volat undique*," I say.

"Love is everywhere," Mairī Lin translates. She looks ready to slide her arm into mine. I step away.

"Are you afraid I've cooked up a touch-based toxin, or are you scared of girls?" she asks.

"I don't owe you any explanations for my boundaries," I snap. I clench my fingers into fists, preparing for her to mock me like everybody else who seems ready to ignore the lessons of poison, plagues, and viral outbreaks past. My armor should protect me from microbial attack, but for every countermeasure I contrive, a Pink Queen like her is surely devising a workaround. To my surprise, she makes no attempt to wound me with her words.

"Noted," she inclines her head and clasps her hands behind her back.

A purple Dahomey lands in front of us, tussling with one of my battle bots. We step over them as they tear each other's heads off.

"You like opera?" I ask Mairī Lin as we walk toward the music.

I should punch her again, yet I don't. Instead, my clenched fingers unfurl. Does she have mind-control tech? My helmet is insulated with neurowave deflectors so even if she's trying to hypno-manipulate me, she can't, which means the only thing holding me back from striking her is me.

Genetrix is thankfully busy leading a battalion against a dozen construction tanks; otherwise, I'd get an earful about letting a pretty robot turn my head.

I need to learn as much about Mairī Lin as I can, I assure myself defensively. *That's why I'm playing along.*

Yet, instead of focusing on Mairī Lin, I find myself humming along to the song. A building topples behind us in a cloud of dust. The melody grows louder; we're getting closer to the source. That soprano voice, so young and fresh, so innocent to the harsh ways of the world—

"It can't be," I murmur.

Mairī Lin claps excitedly. "You recognize it, don't you?"

I do, of course I do, yet I shake my head in bewildered bafflement. Of all the unlikely, near impossible things I've been forced to accept today—my mystery nemesis is Mairī Lin Monroe, psyche transfers to robots is now a thing, she likes my memoirs—this audiograph is the most unbelievable.

"This is a fake," I insist. It has to be.

"We are all of us stars," she replies, "and we deserve to twinkle. Do you know who said that?"

I shake my head, forgetting to pretend I know everything.

"But you do know who's singing this," she says.

"It's me," I reply, "a long time ago."

"A *very* long times ago," she agrees. "You were performing at your school talent show," she says. "You were so good in tryouts, you beat Trey Chakrabarti and his shirtless acrobatics to be the finale."

"He pretended to congratulate me. Ha!" I laugh. "Mother told me he was dying of envy inside."

"Wow. Your mom's really in your head," Mairī Lin notes.

I pretend not to hear her comment as the music sweeps through me.

Blocked by my helmet, I can't wipe away the bubbles of tears in my eyes. The internal environment controls weren't designed for crying, but they manage to dehumidify enough for me to see. The remaining salt burns a bit.

"It's rapturous," Mairī Lin says.

"I was a mere conduit for the song."

"That's your favorite moment, isn't it?" she asks. "The one you're afraid to go back in time to revisit."

I don't deny it.

"Where, how, did you get this recording?" I ask. "Were you there? Were we schoolmates?"

"Oh, goodness no," she laughs, tossing her safety vest onto the head of one of my destroyed bots, "but wouldn't that have been a hoot?"

I wonder if it might have been at that.

"The Gladyses were obsessed with learning everything they could about you; they scoured every database they could find to assemble a profile. We knew you and Caitlin were classmates, so that helped narrow the search. Still, we almost missed this. You weren't introduced by your real name—"

"I was already playing around with alter egos," I say.

"But the Saras' keen ears were able to pick out and extrapolate your eight-year-old singing voice with 89 percent certainty. Team effort. There's a video, too. Want to see?"

We've escaped most of the fighting. Pistol, laser fire, and explosions echo in the distance behind us.

Do I want to see that performance from so long ago? It pulls at me, calling for me to return. I know the dangers of going back to that moment, but to watch it, surely that is safe. Perhaps it's the one thing that can rid me of this incurable itch to relive that sublime instance.

I nod as if in a trance.

"Show me."

Her eyes glow, and a hologram forms of a younger me—a *much* younger me.

I'm dressed in what can only be described as operatic drag. I wear a plastic, horned helm atop a synthetic blond wig woven into two long ponytails; a ghastly amount of rouge reddens my cheeks; a silver-painted breastplate made of chicken wire and papier-mâché makes me look busty.

I'm painfully aware of all the flaws, yet somehow, this one time only, they add to the perfection.

My younger self expertly sings "♪♫ *Amor volat undique.*" It's mesmerizing. I truly was a channel for something grander than myself.

When the song ends, I watch myself take a bow before an audience gone mute. I still remember how those few seconds of silence felt like an eternity—until, now as then, comes the applause. It's wondrous thunder in my ears. The angle of the recording device changes, swiveling to capture the spectators. They stand, every one of them. The angle swings back to young me; plastic roses land on the stage.

I quiver. Seeing this, hearing it, omnipresent invisible hooks that slumbered fitfully wake from their hibernation, growling and sinking deeper into every cell of my body, tugging at me urgently to go back.

Just once, I think. *I can control myself this time.*

Rule number three, I remind myself with a force of will I struggle to possess, *rule number three*.

I feel myself ready to capitulate when the hologram of my performance fades.

Bring it back! a part of me wants to shout.

Delete it! another part of me cries in my mind.

Caught in this seesaw state, I unthinkingly follow Mairī Lin's shapely form toward an archway of pulsing purple mineral deposits.

"In here," she says.

She leads me down stone stairs slick with dripping water and carpeted with black moss that's been carbonized by my/our death ray. I should be taking note of the after-effects of my handiwork, but I'm murmuring the opera tune instead.

Stop it! a part of me orders in my head—a part that sounds too much like Genetrix

No, I respond petulantly.

You know it's a trigger, she answers with her usual bossiness.

I don't care, I shout back.

So many years of self-control, all gone.

We emerge into a subterranean cavern. Mairī Lin claps her hands, releasing a perfectly pitched vibration that runs through the dark crevasse. Crystal formations in every hue of the rainbow vibrate and glow, emitting colored light and a warbling tune.

I hold my inhale; the display is the definition of breathtaking.

"I love gardens," Mairī Lin explains. "After you destroyed all life on the planet, I found a way to grow one. Welcome to my crystal conservatory."

She stops before a rainbow-hued, crystal statuette of a petite girl with a classically pretty face. Her crystal dress cascades downward and outward, seemingly the origin of all the other crystal formations around us. A giant blue sapphire necklace hangs about her neck. She gazes upwards, her beautiful features locked in a scream; her death cry, I assume.

"This is Tourmaline," Mairī Lin says. "We were frenemies before I was locked away. Your death ray killed the biological parts of her brain, but her crystal body remains."

"*Our* death ray," I correct.

"Are you sharing credit or splitting blame?" Mairī Lin winks. She leans in to touch my shoulder but thinks better of it and withdraws her hand. I note the effort.

"Tourmaline's mind is gone," Mairī Lin explains, "but her crystalline body lives on—in a way. Her nervous, circulatory, and digestive systems have all turned to dust. But, with a few electro pulses, I was able to stimulate her mindless matrix into growing and spreading in *very* specific ways."

Mairī Lin unhooks the jewel from around Tourmaline and hands it to me. I accept it, confused. Mairī Lin holds up the back of her blond hair.

"Be a dear and put that on me," she says.

I comply, but only to give myself more time to figure out my next move. I fumble with the clasp but finally get it to click around her neck. I step back. The sapphire sits between her shiny pink breasts.

"What can I say?" she shrugs. "I'm a material girl."

She says this as if it has private meaning.

"A dead world doesn't have to be an ugly world," I say. "The whole idea is to remake everything—*properly*."

"I agree!" she smiles.

"It *is* beautiful," I admit.

"Beautiful enough for you to lower your guard," she says breathily.

A Dahomey's purple, muscled form jumps from behind a crystal stalagmite. She throws a spear of glittering diamond. My suit's shielding engages, the projectile easily penetrates my defenses, and my armor's auto-reflexes kick in, catching the spear before it can stab me through the heart.

I fire a missile that blows the Dahomey to pieces. As purple body parts fill the air, another Dahomey's hand springs from a placid underground lake, grabs my ankle, and yanks me underwater. The purple lady-maton rips off my visor. Freezing water engulfs me, filling my suit. She stabs a crystal into my throat.

Before it slices my jugular, my psyche jumps back in time, aiming for my body that was ten minutes ago, to when Mairī Lin and I stood at the archway leading into this cave. I prepare myself to grab and snap her pink neck, but I never reach my intended moment. My rewinding psyche is jerked like a running dog on a tether; I stop less than a minute in the past.

That's not possible! I rage. My jumps aren't always precise, but the danger lies in overshooting; I've never *under*shot before.

I stand on the edge of the freezing pool of water. Purple body parts fly through the air from the Dahomey I blew up; a flaming purple hand lands next to me. I stumble back before the Dahomey in the pool can grab me, but no hand emerges from the water.

Mairī Lin giggles as I look around in confusion. I fire an explosive into the pool of water just to be sure; water blows into the air, but no purple body parts. Mairī Lin's time-sensitive—does that extend to her robot forms? Evidence would indicate so as she uses her déjà vu to change the course of events. I fire three missiles at her. With impossible movements, she evades them.

"I'm nimbler than the Dahomeys, and my core processor is far more advanced," she taps her temple. "I have to have some kind of advantage if we ever have a serious disagreement."

The missiles hit the cavern wall; the concussive explosions throw us both off our feet. A giant crystal shard drops from the ceiling, slams into my armor, and pins me to the ground.

The weight makes it hard to breathe. In my mind, it takes a millisecond for me to turn an imaginary key and press the time-jump button on my inner master control; the quantum matrix in my brain revs, chokes, and sputters. I remain trapped by the shard *and* in the present.

The crystals, I realize in horror. *They must be inhibiting my powers.*

I look around in panic. The gems are everywhere!

I have to get out of here!

I repeatedly punch at the glittering boulder that's holding me; it cracks in half. I jump free and run for the entrance. I wait for temporal-inhibiting goo to erupt from the glittering material all around like it did from the crystals embedded in the battle stars, but perhaps that required the living portions of Mairī Lin's frenemy's power.

I think that boon will save me until a Dahomey lands in front of me; she stabs a diamond blade toward my chest. My armored arm deflects the piercing weapon, and the glowing disc on my chest blasts her away. She twitches on the ground, her neck and limbs at awkward angles.

My sensors beep. All around, purple Dahomeys emerge from hiding places in the chamber, walking out of pools of water and from refracting alcoves. They're armed with pistols, crystal shards, and laser sabers. They surround me, closing in.

A childhood memory batters me, of being on the playground, of a group of bullies wanting the new calculator I'd won at a computing competition. I've never been as terrified until now.

"I've been intrigued by you since you successfully stole the plans for my death ray," Mairī Lin says. "And the way you used flying saucers to build it on the moon! So creative. I wish we could've gotten to know each other better."

The Dahomeys point their pistols and power up their laser sabers.

I'm dead I'm dead I'm ...

The entire cavern shakes, throwing me and the lady-matons off our feet. Crystals rain down from the quaking cave as dozens of my boring machines erupt from below and drop nimbly from above. Their metal tentacles grab and smash Dahomeys every which way. The purple robots swarm the tanks like army ants, ripping off their coils and plating.

The tanks fire, blasting purple Dahomeys to pieces and rocking the chamber. Crystal shards fall, crushing lady-matons and tanks alike. When the sparkling dust settles, only Mairī Lin and I remain standing.

I'm battered and bruised. She's charred and dripping gooey blue fluid from scores of blast holes.

The smoking remains of our armies surround us amidst shattered crystals.

"Well," Mairī Lin sighs, "it looks like we'll have to call it a draw. But I'll get you yet. You've never met anyone with a brain like mine."

With that, a broken purple lady-maton explodes next to me; the force smashes me into a wall. I shake my head. A whine builds in the rest of the fallen fighters.

"Oh no," I murmur. I fly toward the exit as more Dahomeys self-destruct, knocking me left and right. I spin as crystals fall all around me. My autopilot tries to maneuver around them, but a glittering shard stabs into my jet pack. I crash into the stairs. The whole chamber's falling in.

I stumble toward the exit.

I'm not going to make it!

The archway's collapsing—until Genetrix, beaten and covered in scorch marks, wig askew, steps under the caving construct and pushes it up. The bot can't hold it for long; her gears grind and fly off; pistons pop and belch steam.

I rush past and into the open air.

The bot bleeps at me—even now she's a critic!—and is crushed under a ton of rock.

"Yes, Genetrix," I pant, "that could've gone better."

I look around at the techno carnage of our armies laid to waste. I'm tempted to backflash, but what's the point? Mairī Lin will just see me coming. I must defeat her in the here and now.

It takes hours, but my battered jetpack gets me to my ocean base. I open my cupboard of keys and take out dozens of them, slamming them into slots in my master control panel as quickly as I can. I turn them one after the other, firing up my on-shore fabrication plants, making them work round the clock to churn out newer and better fighter robots, more aggressive tanks with double the number of tentacles, and, in space, my flying saucers begin assembling a mega-bot. Surely, Mairī Lin is regrouping her own forces.

I stick and turn a rose key in one of my bots; it transforms into my new Genetrix. She immediately tells me everything I did wrong today as she helps me out of my battered armor. I could reprogram her to only be supportive or put her on mute, but she's right. She's right about everything. I don't admit that, of course. I deserve the berating, but I'm not going to willingly contribute to making her even more overbearing than she already is.

She throws the pieces of my busted suit and rocket pack into a cart and chirps shrilly.

"Well," I snap back, "if you'd done a better job of protecting me in the first place, I never would've been in danger!"

The bot whines and hands me a Twinkie. I grab it and stuff it into my mouth. She's frustrating, but she does take care of me in a way my other bots can't. The sugar rushes into my adrenalin-crashing body.

"Yes," I agree, "I know you're the only woman I can trust. Who do you think programmed you to remind me?"

She bleeps.

"No, I am *not* fascinated by Mairī Lin." Although who could reasonably blame me if I were?

Genetrix bleeps condescendingly.

"I am a winner!" I insist. I shiver in my onesie. Genetrix puts a cozy blanket over my shoulders.

"Thank you," I say grudgingly.

I look at my monitors as robot soldiers, jets, and tanks emerge from my factories.

"Mark my words, Genetrix, I am going to tear that pink harridan harpy to pieces and weld her decapitated heads together for my new throne!"

Part II

Chapter 8

Genetrix helps me into a velour robe with a wolf head stole, then I walk to the platform with my marble work slab and prepare to be a genius. I grab Mairī Lin's head, the one I dissected after she invaded my library, and try to make sense of it. Hours later, I'm no closer to understanding her tech than when I began. I cram her innards back inside her cranium and shove the casing into Genetrix's arms.

"Get this out of my way," I bark. "I'm going to create something grander than anything this world has ever seen, and I don't need her to do it!"

I rub my palms together as my bots come over an arching bridge, pushing hovercarts with a slew of tech I've stolen over the years but was too timid to try. No longer! My new armor shall be the deadliest any villain has ever devised!

It will have to be. Mairī Lin is unlike any foe I've faced. While I work feverishly on my battle shell, I've no doubt she and her so-called Gladyses, Saras, and Dahomeys are most assuredly plotting and scheming my downfall.

I work well into the night, welding, soldering, programming,

and cursing—I'm too slow; the tech is too banal; the design is hack-
neyed; she'll never be impressed by this or me. Will I have to
rewind to spare myself the humiliation of her seeing this garbage?

Eventually, exhaustion overtakes me. Genetrix cradles me and
flies me up to the nest, where I sleep fitfully in my egg-shaped bed.
Dreams of revenge churn in my mind, and every creak of my ocean
base makes me sit up in anticipation of an attack.

And yet, days, weeks, then months pass, and there's no sign of
my foe. My satellites and scouts can't detect any indication that
she's regrouping.

"Do you think she blew her last fuse?" I ask Genetrix.

The bot scoffs.

"I was smart enough to build you," I reply. "But I agree. We
haven't seen the last of Mairī Lin Monroe."

Meanwhile, my army has tripled in size and ferocity. I watch
with satisfaction as my flying saucers complete my giant warbot and
set its dormant form in geosynchronous orbit around the globe,
ready to come crashing down wherever, whenever I need it.

Genetrix looks at the image of the massive bot curled into a ball
and bleeps at me.

"No, I'm not overcompensating."

She shrugs skeptically.

"Oh, what do you know? Don't answer that!" She dutifully
remains silent.

Of all my new techno-terrors, the most wonderful of all is my
latest armor. After all my near-crippling doubt, I must say, it is
magnificent—not that I have any clue when I'll get to use it. My
drone network has yet to detect any indication of Mairī Lin's return
nor where she's hiding.

So, while I don't believe she's gone, I do feel sufficiently
prepared to allow myself a break on one special day.

I dress in pure pomp—brown leather top hat with a black
feather at the back and flight goggles perched at the front; a vest
stitched with geometric detailing and studded with military medals

that once belonged to one Napoleon Bonaparte; a billowing shirt highlighted by a red ascot about my neck; pants that flare around my thighs and squeeze tight around my calves; boots with buckles running up the sides, and a leg brace of cogs and pistons.

I stand before a gilded full-length mirror.

"Exquisite," I say with delight.

The laboratory lights dim as I descend a semi-circular staircase and sit in a brown leather wingback chair cradled in a rounded glass half-sphere held up by gold spider legs with bulbous joints. Stringed balloons rise from the master control panel behind me, and streamers festoon swooping ramps.

Genetrix carries a silver platter with a giant Twinkie on it; she carefully protects the flame of a single candle with one hand and sings a bleeping, robo-harmonics rendition of "Happy birthday."

The robot sets the tray on a foldout table in front of me. I twiddle my fingers villain style (one of my favorite affectations), make a wish in my fight against Mairī Lin, and blow out the candle. Genetrix hands me a large spoon and a stem glass of synthetic milk.

"Begin the movie!" I shout imperiously.

Genetrix turns a key in my control board, and a hologram forms before me.

You've earned this moment, I assure myself, and take a bite of Twinkie.

The screening was created long ago, before those with special powers and those without fought for global supremacy. It's the story of a "weatherman" who goes to a small colony for "Groundhog Day," a yearly rite that revolves around a mutant rodent with the precognitive ability to determine when winter will turn to spring.

The screening approaches one of my favorite parts—when the weatherman Manifests time-traveling abilities that bear similarities to, and differences from, my own.

I smile as the weatherman wakes in his past for the first time; he looks about in confusion and denial—I know that feeling. I scoop a mouthful of Twinkie, making sure to get a good glob of white filling, and stuff it into my mouth. The clock-radio alarm in the weatherman's rented room hits 6:00 AM and starts playing a pop song.

"♪♪ I got you, babe …" I sing along—until the weatherman's holo-image fizzles out.

"*Deodamnatus*," I swear. The holo projector's acting up again.

I lower my utensil, get up, and adjust several switches on my *dominus imperium*, but instead of fixing the picture, a completely different screening appears—one I'm unfamiliar with. It's black and white, which means it's even older than the time-traveling weatherman story.

The scene that appears features a pair of individuals who I believe bear the XY chromosome but who present as women in dated, female-gendered clothing.

"What is this?" I ask.

Genetrix bleeps in response.

"What do you mean unknown?" I demand. "If it's in my data bank—"

"It's not from *your* data bank, silly; it's from mine," a voice that is both babyish and seductive coos.

My head snaps toward a dais on my left. Mairī Lin's decapitated cranium sits on a rounded bench, poking out from under my carefully folded charcoal polymer shell, almost as if Genetrix were trying to hide the pink remains.

"Isn't the screening wonderful!" Her head vibrates, slowly moving her out from under the fabric.

I stride across a ramp and face her. Above me, a series of floating metal circles rotate about each other. She glances longingly at her blond hair lying next to her, wilted and crushed by the golem skin.

"How are you talking to me?" I demand. "I wiped your motherboard and disconnected any remote linkages."

"Well, I guess you didn't do a very good job," she giggles, "because here I am."

The black and white screening continues.

"I love this part!" she says. "Turn me around so I can see."

"I will do no such thing!" I snap.

I yank my napkin from my collar and place the cloth over her bald head.

"Hey!" she cries. "Now I can't see anything. What's the big idea?"

At my master control, I check my proximity sensors. There's no sign of an attack on the way. I flip switches and turn dials to run a diagnostic. It confirms that Mairī Lin's hacked my entertainment subdirectory. Fortunately, my vital systems remain secure behind more robust firewalls. I type quickly, crafting subroutines to expunge her, but, fast as I am, she counters my every keystroke. I change tactics, creating a series of adaptive codes to keep her quarantined to my screenings database until I can figure out how to expel her.

"I haven't lost, and this isn't a draw," I assure her. "This is *my* home; you are *not* welcome, and I *will* find a way to purge you from my systems."

"Are you still cross that I tried rebuilding one of your cities?" she asks. Her tone is an oddly alluring mix of soothing mother crossed with soliciting sex worker.

"I shall name it *Civitas Planeta*," I shout, sticking and turning keys in the panel with one hand while pulling toggles and adjusting sliders with the other. "It means—"

"World Capital," she translates for me. "Well, I'm going to call it Megalopolis."

Going to? She hasn't given up!

My fingers curl around a joystick.

"You know, there are literally thousands of abandoned cities for you to redo. Can't you let me have just that one?" she says from under my napkin.

"No!" I snap. "That's the best of them all!"

"Isn't the weather divine?"

"Yes, it is!" I shout.

"And those mountain! That water!" she coos.

I yank the napkin off her head. "That's *my* view and *my* micro-climate! Your alloy and gears and whatever that sludge is running through your veins can't even enjoy it."

"It's not about that," she snips.

"Then what's it about?" I demand.

"Not letting *you* have it," she replies.

"That's it!" I snap. "Genetrix, the Box!"

The bot rolls forward with a tech dampening container that looks like an antiquated safe. The bot beeps primly.

"That's right; this *is* where unwelcome guests go," I agree.

"You two have the most enmeshed, unhealthy mother-son relationship I've ever seen," Mairī Lin tsks.

"That's absurd," I snort. "She's my servant, not my—"

"Genetrix means mother in Latin," Mairī Lin counters.

She's impossible!

"Stop ruining my birthday!" I stomp my foot.

"My dear Timematician, I'm *saving* your birthday," she insists.

"*Deliramentum*," I mutter, putting on thick rubber gloves before I take her head in my hands.

"It's not nonsense," she counters. "Who spends their birthday alone when they could spend it with me?"

"Everyone!" I snap.

"You're being a baby," she sighs as I jerk the door of the safe open, shove her inside, and slam it shut. Mechanisms whir and click, locking her away.

Mairī Lin's muffled words fight to get out.

"I can't hear you!" I shout.

She falls silent.

Good!

I return to the master control, grab my plate, and shove a spoonful of Twinkie into my mouth. I toggle, turn, and twist an array of controls.

"*Triumphi!*" I cry as the image of the two gender morphs fades. But my celebratory exclamation is premature. Despite my efforts, the story of the time-traveling weatherman does not return. Instead, a gray-haired man in a silver lab outfit appears.

"Stand aside, you clumsy clump!" he cries. I take his character to be a scientist or doctor of some sort—it takes one to know one, I suppose. He's hitting and berating a rounded robot with tubular arms and pincer hands.

"What is this?" I ask. The robot's design is terribly impractical, but I am drawn to the overall aesthetic with its donut-shaped head and anachronistic styling of what a robot might look like. With a few modifications—

Genetrix interrupts my thoughts, responding to my confusion with the coded bleeps for "unknown" and "error."

"Quiet you …!"

I pause in mid-yell, recalling and repeating the words of the scientist in the screening. "You clumsy clump."

Not bad, I think.

The holo image of the unfamiliar screening warbles and vanishes, stealing the disparaging doctor and his pinhead partner from sight.

"Where are you going?" I shout. "Come back!" I'm about to turn to my controls to force the feed to resume when my gaze lands on the safe holding what's left of the Mairī Lin that first invaded my lair. Understanding turns the Twinkie in my stomach. I go to the Box, open it, and remove her head.

"Did you like that little teaser?" she asks. "I'll put it back on if you keep me out here. Think of it as a birthday truce."

I grit my teeth. I don't want to concede anything to this metallic minx, but I do want to see the rest of this mystery screening.

"Fine," I say. "For the sake of expediency."

"You are *such* a Dr. Smith!" she says.

"Is that a compliment or an insult?" I ask suspiciously.

"Yes!" she agrees.

I set her head on the foldout table in front of me. The screening resumes. At first, we watch in silence, but that's replaced by laughs. When the episode ends, Mairī Lin asks if I'd like to watch another.

"Yes," I snap with an irritation I don't wholly feel.

After the second episode, we watch a third and a fourth. Genetrix bleeps at me.

"I don't care if it's past my bedtime," I mutter.

Genetrix chirps and scolds.

"You're embarrassing me," I hiss. I press a button on the arm of my chair, and the bot's arms and head drop limply as she powers down.

The screenings don't end that night.

In the weeks that follow, I barely get any work done as Mairī Lin and I consume season after season of the serialized program. Ostensibly, it's about a boring, homogenous white family adrift and misadventuring amidst the farthest reaches of space, but the series would be a write-off if not for the screeching Dr. Smith and his acidic alliterative remarks to the castaways' robot. The doctor is the outsider, yet he steals every scene and makes every episode.

As we watch, I deride Mairī Lin for being a "demented diode." Without missing a beat, she calls me a "despotic dunce."

She giggles; I laugh my wheezing laugh.

By the time we get to the end of the series, I'm dressed in a housecoat and an unkempt beard puffs from my cheeks. Both of us agree to forego watching any of the reboots—it just wouldn't be the same. Outside, the sun rises on a clear day. We were up much of the night—again. I find myself feeling empty now that it's over. I'm tempted to jump back in time to relive it all, but I know better.

Rules one through three, I remind myself.

"If I'd known you before," I say to Mairī Lin, "maybe I wouldn't have destroyed the world."

"Are you getting soft on me?" she asks.

"Never!" I cry imperiously.

We share another laugh.

"Well, there's no turning back time," she sighs.

"Of course, there is," I snort, waving imperiously. "I'm the Timematician."

I wait for her to be pleased that I've accepted the moniker.

"No," she disagrees, "you're not. Not anymore."

I arch a confused brow. "What are you …"

I look out the window; a missile flies toward us.

Chapter 9

The projectile veers downward and out of sight.

"We had a truce!" I shout at Mairī Lin's head.

"A *birthday* truce," she corrects. "Your birthday ended weeks ago."

The missile explodes against the base of my lair. The entire structure shakes, throwing me off my feet, and flames roar through a hole ripped into the bottom of the cubic chamber. Another missile hits; ramp cables snap; the platform I'm on teeters, throwing me over the railing. I fall toward the breach in the floor and the churning waves exposed below.

I try to backflash, but I fumble and fail to get the key in my brain into its imaginary slot. Is it the fear? The sense of shock from yet another betrayal? A belief that I have this coming? From this height, the ocean's surface is going to be like hitting a wall. I smash into it. Breath turns to searing pain that rips through my chest. Have I broken a rib?

The current sucks me under.

Around me sinks my destroyed bots, a pair of cathodes struggling to spark, my master control panel split in two, and a slew of keys with decorative heads.

The cold will kill me in moments; one moment's all I need to rewind and prevent any of this from happening. This time, in one fluid motion, the mental key goes in; I turn it, slam the imaginary activation button, and initiate the jump. I brace for the rewind, and nothing changes. I sink further, and my eyes widen in horror. Beneath me, the mass of sunken warships, planes, and undetonated naval mines on the ocean floor is covered in mountains of glittering crystals.

When did they get there?

A robotic swordfish drifts past, dark and powered down, skewered by a crystal harpoon. A torpedo zooms toward me. Mairī Lin intends to blow me up before I can drown or freeze!

But the torpedo streaks by. Leaving a trail of bubbles in its wake, it dives deeper and explodes against the near-impervious glass of my underwater archives. The force throws me backward and turns my precious collection into deadly projectiles. The pharaoh's sarcophagus, a reclining Buddha, and my gramophone fly at me. Their crushing trajectories barely avoid my battered body.

Water floods the chamber, knocks over shelves, swirls amidst my books and collectibles, and rises around my convertible. The deep-sea diver in the driver's seat is tauntingly within sight yet too far to do me any good. More debris falls from my base above and sinks around me, including boxes of Twinkies and Mairī Lin's bald pink head. Her indented eyes glow.

"I deactivated all your bots. They can't rescue you this time," she says through her near-motionless mouth.

Treasonous tyrant! I silently rage.

"I want you to know, in the end, I really did like you."

My house robe wings around me as I futilely reach for her, wanting to gouge her luminescent eyes. Pain should be coursing through my injured form, but I feel nothing; hypothermia is taking me. Her head slips through my grasp and disappears into a crevice amidst the glittering mounds of crystals below. I try another time jump; I continue to sink.

No! I rage. *This can't be how it ends! It can't!*

I push the switch in my mind harder as if I have nothing and everything to lose, fighting the dampening effects of the crystals with everything I've got. I imagine Genetrix berating me.

I'm filled with a combination of rage at her failing me and a desperate need to prove I don't need her. It fuels me. I forget the key and button, imagining instead a complete overload of my central core. My brain and every nerve in my body feel like they're about to explode from the internal and external pressure.

Something pops inside my skull—an aneurysm, I'm sure—and I'm in the ocean no more.

I stand, safe inside my grand laboratory, my dry robe wrapped around my belly as I inhabit that body in the past; the closing theme song of the dated science fiction show plays from hidden speakers. Mairī Lin's head sits on the fold-out table

"I'm impressed," she says. "The crystals around your base spread here overnight, so they're still maturing and won't reach full strength for a few days, but still, well done! That said, I doubt you can pull off a second backflash."

I dab my nose. It's bleeding. That's never happened from a time jump before. I touch my rib and wince. I don't think it's broken, but I'm certainly bruised. Did I create these injuries by pushing my power beyond its threshold?

From the corner of my eye, I see a missile flying toward us through the clear blue skies.

"I sent it earlier this go around," Mairī Lin confesses.

Why aren't the ballistic countermeasures activating?

For the same reason the proximity alarm isn't sounding. She's gotten past my firewalls and deactivated them. Genetrix remains inert from when I turned her off, and the rest of my bleeping robots are powering down one by one; bunch of dim-witted doormats!

I look at the magnificent suit I constructed to end the lady-matons.

"Armor!" I shout.

"I've deactivated that as well," Mairī Lin says.

My throat runs dry. I try another time jump. The world blurs, then snaps to; I remain anchored in the present. I push harder, as I did in the water, and throw up. My power—it's gone!

I gasp and spit; she giggles—until my rubberized bodysuit, forgotten on a bench, inflates and blasts toward me. We both gape in surprise. The shell opens down the middle and envelopes me protectively. I nearly throw up again as the head and face-shield wrap about me.

"Huh," she says. "I did not see that coming. I really am a dundering dunce. I hacked your *old* gear. This one's never been connected to your mainframe."

It's a tinker project, which means I haven't had a chance to incorporate any of my usual detailing. The helmet lacks anything cool—like mandibles or horns or a malleable brow that can create the impression of imperious disdain for the blithering idiots I've wiped from the earth. Instead, I'm sheathed in a sleek, charcoal, golem-like second skin with a single rounded eyepiece. Thankfully, the voice activation works—even though it was my other armor I was calling to.

"I like the new look," Mairī Lin says.

"I don't care what you think," I shriek. There's no voice modulator, so I sound like me—the real me.

The missile strikes, followed by two more. The explosions throw me into the ocean once more. My suit does its job. I'm warm; I'm safe. Fiery debris, along with Mairī Lin's head, sinks next to me.

I grab her pink countenance between my covered palms.

"I know I already told you this, but I do want you to know, in the end, I really liked you," she squawks as I crush her pink skull.

Chapter 10

Hours later and many leagues away, I clamber out of the ocean onto the shores of a tropical island. My bum knee throbs, and this skinsuit isn't equipped with a heating pad. That is far from the worst of my predicament. In lieu of sand, the beach glitters with crystal sediment that dampens my powers, and crystal vines grow up palm trees petrified long before my death ray washed over the planet.

Through my suit's neural relays, I patch into my network of satellites and confirm what I already suspect. Mairī Lin's crystals stretch to every corner of the globe.

"Very well," I say. "I'll just go to outer space and time jump from there."

The antigravity packs in the soles of my boots blast me upward. I miss the speed and thrust of my rocket pack—and the style.

You'll have it back soon enough, I assure myself. *You'll have it all back.*

I get as far as the stratosphere when my proximity alarm pulses. A missile speeds toward me. Underwater and low to the ground, I can more easily evade my enemy's radar, but at this height, I'm target practice. I accelerate my upward trajectory. I must get up to go back—but I can't gain altitude fast enough.

I try and fail to backflash.

The missile hits me. The explosion pummels me with what feels like a thousand concrete fists all over my body and blows me off course. I fall, recover, and blast skyward. Another missile strikes me head-on from above, throwing me downward. I try again and again to fly beyond the reach of Mairī Lin's crystals. Missiles hit me over and over.

My anti-grav packs falter; I fall. In the distance, a dozen explosive projectiles speed toward me. I bang my heels together and cry, "*Nullum gratuitum prandium est scriptor!*" and my boots flare to life. I no longer fly up; I flee. Sonic booms echo in my wake—to no avail. The missiles are gaining on me. If they hit, I'm done for. I try to shoot them; my blaster jams.

No, no, no!

In the distance, I see the shiny towers of the island city where the Supergenics lived before I ended them. I fly there, the projectiles close on my heels, and I weave amidst skyscrapers dotted with crystals. Several of the missiles hit the buildings and explode, smacking me with burning shrapnel.

I course correct, leaving Supergenic Jupitar Island behind as I whoosh across a river and approach the boroughs where the DNA regulars lived. Dozens of missiles blast after me.

I fly over the squat concrete tenements that dominate this side of the river—a stark contrast to the sky-scraping glass and steel of Jupitar Island.

I have no time to deconstruct the social, class, and resource inequities between the two societies nor the peace treaty that reinforced and institutionalized the divide.

They're all dead anyway, I remind myself. *Do you want to join them?*

I do not.

Beyond the dreg tenements is a rearing fence. Crystals twine like vines over its chain links and create glittering outlines around radiation- and mutant-warning signs. The fence separates the boroughs from one of the cities doomed during the Genetic Wars. Its towers, once tall and proud, now crumble under their own weight and are as dotted with Mairī Lin's glittering crystals as the rest of the planet.

Above, thick black storm clouds rumble and roil. Lightning crackles within the billowing mass, followed by bellowing thunder —a sound I remember from my youth. The storm has been there for as long as I've been alive. It's a leftover of the Genetic Wars.

My sensors show the missiles closing in.

I don't want to do this! I rage at myself—and I fly into the billowing darkness.

For a moment, my sensors go blank, and I'm flying blind until lightning erupts all around me. I weave and dodge. The sizzling energy is like blender blades, ready to shred me like a veggie tossed into one of the morning smoothies Genetrix used to try to force-feed me until I wiped the recipe from her databank.

The missiles lack my maneuverability. Lightning flares and rips through the projectiles; they explode all around me, and the shock-waves throw me out of the clouds. Gravity grips me, sucking me downward. I fall toward the abandoned city battered by wars long before I was born. I crash into—and through—a pile of steel and brick overgrown with glittering crystals—until I hit a foundation strong enough to stay my fall.

My golem suit absorbs the brunt of the impact; I grunt, bounce, then lie there, groaning and wracked by muscle spasms that render me powerless. I wait for another barrage of missiles to finish me. They don't come.

Does Mairī Lin and her demented Dahomeys think me dead?

I wince at the pain. My bum leg throbs more than everything

else. Broken crystals surround me from my crash landing. My suit's spectro vision activates. I struggle to my elbows, tilt my head, and fear I've sustained brain damage because I'm surrounded by walls of comic books, posters of women in bloody armor, and shelves of figurine superhero collectibles.

It takes my battle-addled brain a moment to realize where I am —a comic book store, one from before the wars between humans and Supergenics.

I've come across places like this before in my travels, but I've never seen one so well-preserved. Normally, the comics are faded, torn, and burnt to such a degree that only a few panels remain readable. But this place, aside from a layer of dust, looks as if the shopkeeper locked up the night before and could be back any moment to start another day of sales.

I pick up an issue that my entrance knocked to the floor and gaze at a muscled man in a loincloth, swinging on a vine. Hundreds more titles surround me. In another lifetime, a younger me could've lost himself here for years.

You're not a child, I hear Genetrix beeping in my mind.

"Shut up," I mutter, but she's right.

I need intel. I wince, groan, and force myself to my feet. I set the comic book on a dusty counter next to a set of oddly shaped dice. My monocle projects a holo-map of the planet, showing all of my secret bases in flashing green. One by one, they wink out.

She's destroying them.

My factories flare blue as Mairī Lin takes them over and locks me out of their systems.

"Genetrix!" I shout—but aside from my inner critic, there is no Genetrix.

My gaze lands on a dummy dressed in a military-style, black trench coat. Buttons descend one side of a high collar, over the shoulders, and up the forearms. An explanatory plaque reads, *From The Archivist Wears Black;* it's memorabilia from a screening.

"Do something!" I order. It remains immobile.

I collapse to my knees.

"Please," I beg. "She's taken everything from me."

I pant amidst illustrated covers depicting heroes and villains. Pain wracks my leg, the world swims, and darkness takes me.

Chapter 11

To my disappointment, I wake the next day. Thunder rumbles through the hole I made in the ceiling. Lightning crackles in the ever-present black clouds above, but somehow the storm seems less potent than I recall from my youth.

At some point during the night, I draped a blue and white cape over me as a blanket; my arm is wrapped around the dummy in its archivist coat; I hug it tightly as if to draw strength.

I have no idea who I am anymore; I'm certainly not Dr. Better-Than, not after Mairī Lin's made me flounder my every move in a choreographed game of chess I forgot we were playing.

I gently disengage my arms from the dummy as if fearing to wake it, spot a cane with a question mark on its handle, and use it to struggle to my feet. I flick a switch, and twinkling lights on strings pulse gently.

In a stock/staff room, I find a shopping bag with a tracksuit in it; the price tag's still on. I strip out of my golem-like sheathing and don the outfit. Under the front counter is a first aid kit with an antiquated cellular regenerator. I try to use it to take the ache out of my bruises and joints, but of course, it's out of power.

"Useless!"

I set the dummy upright. It stares and silently berates me as if it were Genetrix.

"I know I'm an idiot!" I shout in response to its unspoken words.

I gnash my jaw as it demands I justify myself.

"Because I thought we were becoming friends!" I yell.

The dummy refuses to shut up.

"Right," I snap, "because who could ever be friends with me?"

If I'm expecting pity, I don't get it, not from this solitude-hardened mannequin, not after what I've done.

"It's her death ray, too," I answer defensively. For a moment, I recall katana woman—Caitlin—turning to ash before me. "Mairī Lin should like me *because* I'm a genocidal maniac. I'm powerful; I'm brilliant; I'm—"

The dummy and I stare at each other.

My lip quivers. "Why would you say that?"

I listen to the silence, wipe away my tears, and nod in defeated acceptance.

"It's true," I agree. "Without my do-overs, I'm nothing."

Neither the dummy nor I have any more to say.

My prototype skinsuit is out of power; I leave it as I hobble out of the below-grade comic shop, wincing as I stumble up a set of stairs leading to a trick door that's cleverly camouflaged amidst the rubble of the surrounding city. Someone went to a lot of trouble to keep this place intact and off the grid. I limp outside.

Lightning crackles, and thunder booms. They don't bother me the way most bright lights and loud noises do. Maybe something to do with the temporal quirk in my brain, or perhaps it's because I grew up with the never-moving storm.

I'm physically buffered from the lightning storm as well. Rearing concrete towers hold glass globes aloft; the orbs draw the lightning toward them, absorbing their power and feeding it into an energy grid for both the boroughs and Jupitar Island. Those globes were on my list of infrastructure to maintain for my own purposes. Now, crystals crawl up the structures. I wonder what will happen when the glittering menace reaches the energy-absorbing globes.

I walk slowly through deserted streets of cracked asphalt and dilapidated buildings, past slender, slowly turning oxygenators, which thankfully continue to function.

I reach the crystal-encrusted chain-link security fence separating this condemned metropolis from the brutalist tenements where the DNA regulars lived. I smack the cover off of a security panel holding a gate shut, easily hotwire the circuits, and the lock clicks open. The gate moves a mere fraction. Crystals have formed over the hinges. I pick a rebar off the ground—*Don't think of the germs, don't think of the germs, don't think of*—and use it to force the barrier open.

I limp through, leaning on the question-mark cane.

It's strange being back in the boroughs. I traverse the orderly streets, some overgrown with crystals, others not yet. I avoid the piles of ash atop clothes littering the street, many of them looking like murder-scene outlines.

In a townhome, I find canned oats, dehydrated veggies, and protein powder supplements that will irritate my bowels but keep me alive. There are no Twinkies on this side of the river; there is bottled water and sanitizer gel. I disinfect my hands a dozen times. On a mantle sits a plastic Viking helmet with horns, tugging at me with memories of days long ago—and of how Mairī Lin used my most cherished memory as a weapon against me. It would be far more comfortable to stay in a proper house than to go back to the comic book store, but I don't dare remain. Being here now is a risk.

I leave the home and helm behind. I do take a floral dress from a closet in the master bedroom.

A few streets over, I break into a maintenance center to grab tarps, tools, and a dozen tubes of All Stick. There's a small space heater, so I filch that too.

I take my haul in a purloined knapsack and a pull cart, and I limp back through the busted city, hoping the electric storm will help hide me from Mairī Lin.

At my new lair, I repair the hole I made in the ceiling when I crash-landed, patching it with rebars, a tarp, the rusted hood of a car, and smaller chunks of concrete. I glue it all together with the quick-sealing All Stick. Crystals are already growing over it.

Over the next several days, I scavenge the dead city around me. I come upon three smashed protector hovercrafts that must've been on patrol when my death ray hit. The tech is primitive by my standards, but I'm able to strip it to cobble together life-sign deflectors for extra protection against Mairī Lin's sensors and to set up security cams, mics, and motion detectors around my comic book base.

I also transform the store's payment counter into a makeshift control panel using ancient computers I've found in the dead city and a round electronic game with four buttons of different colors (red, green, yellow, and blue) that light up with varied sounds in different patterns for users to repeat back (I've dimmed both the audio and bulbs to acceptable levels). It's kitschy cute, and the motherboards from the hovercrafts are what I need to bring my new *dominus imperium* online, saving me from another risky foray into the boroughs.

Little by little, these micro-victories leave me feeling less doomed. The dummy even shares the occasional encouraging word. I've forced it into the purloined floral dress, which has puffy sleeves and a lacy collar that descends over a chest I've turned into a bosom using a bra stuffed with padding. A rose flower broach I found is pinned above one breast, and a white Victorian wig from the comic book store's costume section rises in a tall updo with curls dangling over her shoulders.

I wire into the power absorbers above to recharge the cellular regenerator, my golem suit, and to run my growing collection of salvaged tech. Sitting in a lawn chair, I tap on an antiquated type board that lacks the nuanced keys of the language I created and gaze at a single cracked video monitor. It's enough for me to hack into Mairī Lin's maze of data networks.

The green light on the circular game lights up as I breach her first portal of security. A rush of energy flows through me. Victory is around the corner—until I hit firewall after firewall. The yellow light flashes and honks.

Damnare! I curse.

The dummy glares at me condescendingly.

"Just settle down, Mother. I mean, Genetrix."

I type with the ferocity of a tiger taking down a gazelle—I saw that in an old nature show once—and I find a rare gap in Mairī Lin's security.

"*Triumphi!*" I cry to the suddenly flashing green light—prematurely as it turns out. I've penetrated a low-security, sub-sub folder (with many more subs). It contains a spreadsheet of her assets, the asset's current operational status, and timelines for target output and resource extraction goals.

While I love a good spreadsheet (though not as much as a Venn diagram; there's something about those overlapping circles that speak to me), this document fills me with the opposite of joy. The longer I watch it change with real-time updates, the more it highlights the bleakness of my situation in columns and rows that feel less wondrously orderly and more brutally doomsday.

Not only has Mairī Lin destroyed my various bases (as indicated in column D), she's quickly repurposing my infrastructure for world domination (column F). My robot-building factories are working full-throttle—for her; she's looted my armament stockpiles, coopted my dormant mega-bot in orbit, and locked me out from my death ray on the moon.

Her death ray, Genetrix corrects.

Indeed. Mairī Lin has stolen it back.

I wash down a gritty nutrition bar with a grittier shake. My stomach churns, and I rush to a camping potty I've set up next to a cardboard cutout of a cartoon duck drinking a beer in an easy chair.

While my digestion unravels, so does the rest of me. My entire body shakes as I sob into my hands. When the tears run dry, I'm more exhausted than before. I wipe my bottom with abrasive toilet paper, pull up my track pants, and squirt disinfectant into my hands.

I should kill myself.

The green light on the circular game I've attached to my master control panel winks out; the red one awakens, pulling me from my dark thoughts. Something's triggered my ad hoc security system. On the cracked monitor, I watch a squadron of Gladyses, Saraswatis, and a single Dahomey land outside the comic book store.

They've found me! I realize. Relief overshadows fear. I did my best; it wasn't enough. Finally, this grueling torture I'm enduring can end.

I wait for the Dahomey to burst through the ceiling, pointing her pistol at me and filling my chest with photon blasts while her laser saber separates my head from my neck.

Moments pass, and the Dahomey remains above ground, keeping a watchful eye as the Gladyses carry tools toward a tall tubular mechanism covered in vents.

"An oxygenator," I murmur. They're going to destroy it, along with the rest of the network all over the planet. It's an elegant if vicious plan. Without the devices converting CO^2 to oxygen, I'll suffocate. Mairī Lin and her lady-matons will be done with me at last—and there's nothing I can do to stop them.

I take a few deep breaths, enjoying the sensation while I can. I watch but barely see the lady-matons work. I'm too busy pondering what I could've and should've done differently.

The Gladyses unscrew panels—no doubt planting explosives within the device—and then swap out a grungy old air filter for a new one. The Gladyses screw the panels back into place, leaving the air converter in better shape than they found it. A Saraswati chips off a few stray crystals that have attached to the oxygenators while the other orange lady-matons close their eyes.

They touch their pinky and ring fingers to their thumbs. I recognize the gesture from raiding Buddhist and Hindu temples of yore. If I recall my research correctly, this configuration is called the Prana Mudra. It's hard to say over the sound of thunder from the storm above, but I think the Saras are humming.

At first, I wonder if they're meditating, but then I realize this isn't some spiritual nonsense. Despite the poor angle of my camera, I clearly see the crystals around the oxygenator retract.

Do vibrations affect the crystal lattice?

I tuck the theory into a mental folder for further analysis, for a more immediate question is in need of answer. I lean closer to the monitor. I can do some of the most advanced quantum calculus there is, so I know this basic math doesn't add up. Why are the lady-matons doing maintenance on the oxygenators? The crystals don't need air—I've run a few tests. So why would the lady-matons need a breathable atmosphere? Does Mairī Lin have plans to repopulate the planet somehow? I adjust the volume control and listen to what they're saying.

"I don't see why we're bothering," the Dahomey says.

My thoughts exactly.

"Maybe one day our organic body will be ambulatory and off the ventilator," a Gladys responds. "I've been devising some promising treatments. I also want to restart my cloning program to grow ourselves bio-bodies. It's a pity the Timematician destroyed all my embryos with our *mors trabem*."

"Don't call it that. It's a death ray. And I don't want to be organic," the Dahomey says, flexing her powerful arms. "I like this form. You should focus on finding a way to make us independent of our weakling birth body."

"Well, Mairī Lin wants—" the Gladys starts to say.

"Mairī Lin doesn't know what's good for her," Dahomey interrupts. Lightning flashes dangerously close to them, making them all flinch.

"Hurry up," the Dahomey says, glancing nervously at the rumbling lightning storm.

"All done," the Gladys replies. They nod to each other, bend their knees, jump into the air, and fly off.

I plonk into a duct-taped chair. Dummy Genetrix and I stare at each other. I can't have heard them correctly, can I?

"Mairī Lin's biological body is still alive."

Twist!

"She must've inoculated her organic form before our death ray destroyed all other life on the planet."

Was it her insufferable déjà vu that prompted her to do so? Was it a matter of course when she first invented the device? Whatever the case, according to Dahomey, Mairī Lin needs her biological body to keep the lady-matons functioning.

"Which means … I can kill her."

But how?

I pace among the aisles of comic books, my brilliant brain abuzz. Begone my morose, brooding, death-wish self! There is work yet to be done after all. I consider scheme after scheme.

"No," I mutter to myself, discarding idea upon idea, "not good enough; against her? Be serious!"

Mairī Lin is truly the wiliest of creatures. To destroy her, I must …

My thoughts stop as my eyes land on a comic book version of the series she introduced me to about the mincing scientist and his robotic sidekick adrift in space. I pull it free.

In it, the scientist is using sleight of hand to delight the dullard family he's stuck with.

"It's all about misdirection," I realize. My heart pounds harder —not with fear, but with excitement. I have the beginnings of a wonderfully wicked plan.

To destroy Mairī Lin, I must do what she did to me; I must

distract her. But how? With what? I rove through the comic book store, seeking inspiration to design a stratagem of destruction unlike any that's come before. I stop in a section devoted to posters for old screenings. The posters are coated in plastic adhered to cardboard backings and housed in a trio of bins. I flip through them until I reach a print of a winking, busty, blond white woman in a scanty black evening dress; she's held up by two frumpy-by-comparison gender morphs in dated dresses.

"I recognize you," I say. Admittedly, the image is not a twin to Mairī Lin. My nemesis has metallic fuchsia "skin" while the actress' bio flesh is pale white. Nor are the facial features an exact match. But the hair? The bust line? Identical. It's as if Mairī Lin is paying homage to this icon through an avatar, but perhaps maintaining something of herself as well, finding the overlaps but honoring the distinctions.

Like a Venn diagram.

Or I'm wrong, and there's no connection whatsoever between the woman in the graphic and the one who is trying to end me. Doubt gnaws at me until I see the name of the lead actress emblazoned at the top of the poster. My remedial math skills kick in as I put two and two together.

"Mairī Lin Monroe," I whisper, "you've handed me the variables and constants of your own destruction."

Chapter 12

My brand of genius is uniquely suited to the task ahead. I am a man of formulae, and this is the most important calculation of my life.

$x+y=a$. If a is annihilation, solve for x and y.

I start with x.

I don my recharged golem suit and seek out war tech, scavenging not only the battleground of the doomed city I now call home but also the labs of DNA regulars and Supergenics alike. I find plenty of components, bringing them back to the comic book store where I begin to assemble a new battle suit to smite Mairī Lin and her other parts.

I thread, I solder, I polish, bringing it to life, day by day.

But the how of defeating Mairī Lin is in the y.

I grab a novelty pencil and notepad from a shelf and begin writing down all the co-factors I can think of—including every stray word or offhand reference Mairī Lin has made, from the name of her brain-dead crystal frenemy to the time she called herself "a material girl." That meant something, I'm sure of it, but what? The list grows. Each bullet point is a potential weakness I aim to exploit. I gaze at my inventory of *y;* I *will* turn this variable into a constant!

To gain insight into her twisted mind and to test a growing theory, I attempt to hack into her entertainment database. I fail until I follow her digital trail to an external archive from before the Genetic Wars known as a "streaming service" that's virtually open-source.

I prepare to create an algorithm to sort through the mass of popular culture, but Mairī Lin's saved me the time. She has a "profile," which includes a coquettish photo of her pink-self laughing gaily alongside a publicly accessible collection of all her favorite screenings. Who would ever share such information for everyone to see?

Someone who believes herself alone on this planet. It's almost too delicious.

At night, when my back aches too much to work on my battle suit, I sit on a loveseat to pursue my anti-Mairī Lin research; I've removed dummy Genetrix's legs so she can sit at my side; her dress flops over the edge of the cushion. We watch the historical-cultural material that's key to my enemy's defeat—Mairī Lin's movie playlist.

The screenings she favors have the strangest titles and stranger plots, from elixirs of youth gone wrong to the preference of high-class men for fair-follicled women as objects of attention. I wear the striped cape, eat a bag of microwaved popped corn, and drink a can of warm soda as I memorize every gesture and line.

I mouth along with the blond actress who inspired Mairī Lin's namesake as she talks about her "thing" for saxophone players. I silently recite how all it takes is a few bars of 'Melancholy Baby' to turn the character's spine to custard.

I'll turn Mairī Lin's vertebrae to jello, I think. I press pause on a remote, pick up a polaroid camera, and take a photo of the frozen scene. The camera makes a *vuh-zimf* sound and fills the air with a chemical smell. I flutter the photo to help it develop, then pin it to a wall full of my research. Colored yarn links a slew of items to each other. I set Genetrix onto her dummy legs and stand next to her as we take it all in.

"Follow the pattern," I tell my silent companion. "See here?" I walk to the wall and tap side-by-side photos.

On the left is the blond actress Mairī Lin loves; on the right is a pop songstress from a later decade. They wear nearly identical satin dresses; both are surrounded by hunks in tuxedos showering them in diamond jewelry.

"*This* is the material girl connection!" I say triumphantly.

Genetrix is not so easily convinced that I'm on to anything.

"No, I am not crazy!" Well, perhaps a little at this point, but I'm not going to admit that to her. "Stop putting my neurodiversity into a straitjacket!"

She's as infuriating as ever.

"Just listen for once instead of criticizing all the time. I know I'm socially awkward, but I'm *not* a child! I *do* know what I'm talking about."

I slide my finger along a string that leads from the material girl photo to a polaroid of a scene from another of the videographs that's part of Mairī Lin's most-watched collection. It's not a full-length screening; in fact, at 5:01 minutes, it's quite short and is cataloged under the classification "music video."

"Look here! In *this*," I tap the image, "the songstress expresses herself by grabbing her crotch and having simulated intercourse with a muscular factory worker."

Genetrix stares at me reproachfully.

"I am not being a pervert, and I do have a point!" I snap. "Let me finish! You're always interrupting. The imagery in this music video isn't wholly original." I follow a strand away from the crotch-grabbing songstress to a poster of a cybernetic entity with feminized features. She sits on a throne-like chair in front of a pentagram on a wall. Diodes are attached to a semi-circular helm about her temples while bands of energy encircle her form. "Based on archival analysis, I believe the songstress is paying homage to this—the first-ever feature-length 'science-fiction' film."

I jab my fingers into the abdomen of the cyborg on the poster, careful to avoid her chest area. I sometimes think Genetrix is the pervert given her obsession with body parts. A piece of paper is tacked beneath the cybernetic character. In my neat handwriting is a key phrase from the film.

Without the heart, there can be no understanding between the hand and the mind!

I *will* find a way to use that quote against my enemy.

"The story takes place in a utopic metropolis built overtop a vast machine complex that relies upon a dystopian mass of workers to keep it running," I explain. "*This* is where Mairī Lin got the inspiration for her lady-matons *and* to call her city Megalopolis. The film's retro-futuristic industrialized aesthetic is frankly more my style than hers, but I digress."

Genetrix stares at my collection of images connected by threads.

"You see it now, too, don't you?"

I step away from my Mairī Lin map, stand next to Genetrix, and rub my hands together.

"It's all so obvious; the dots practically connect themselves. Mairī Lin Monroe, I'm coming for you and your cybernetic army too."

Chapter 13

The next day, in my comic book lair, dummy Genetrix and I gaze at a countertop lacquered with black and white comic book pages. Upon it lies my new suit, arms and legs sticking out from under a satiny cape draped over it.

My skin itches, and not just from the use of substandard soaps and toilet paper. I'm dying to put on my magnificent creation.

"Soon," I assure myself. I speak true because time is running out.

The Dahomeys have begun destroying the food stores they find, and the crystals are starting to spread indoors, crushing and hardening over canned goods I might otherwise subsist on. It's getting harder and harder to scavenge even basic rations. My stomach growls hungrily.

I know, I think. *I'm hungry, too.*

Even if I defeat Mairī Lin—*If?* I berate myself. *When!*—there may be nothing left for me to live off of. Perhaps the crystals could be converted into a nutrient supplement, but this is hardly my area of expertise—which means I can't simply best her in the *now*. I need my power back to beat her in the *then*.

I don my barebones golem suit. It auto-tightens to fit my shrinking belt-line and to support my leg. What the charcoal shell lacks in pizzazz, it makes up for in practicalities—stealth, speed, and its ability to take a beating.

"Good day," I incline my head to Genetrix, who is thankfully silent in my head this morning.

When I creep out of my comic book lair, I have to smash the crystals that have formed over the hidden outer door. If I wait much longer, the day will come when they've grown too thick for me to break out, or the Dahomeys, Gladyses, and Saraswatis will notice the busted shards I'm creating and will discover my lair. Either way, the comic book store is on the cusp of becoming my tomb.

The time traveler is officially on a ticking clock.

I fly low to the ground through the broken city that's almost unrecognizable under a layer of glitter. Many of the oxygenators now have an orange Saraswati next to it, eyes closed, their quartet of hands in the Prana Mudra formation, humming and vibrating gently. Even so, the crystals fight to creep over their feet and the base of the oxygenators.

The orange lady-matons ignore me. I think it's taking all of their concentration to keep the crystals at bay.

When I reach Restitution River, I dive through a thin layer of crystal that's formed over the surface like the first layer of ice on a winter's day. Within the churning waters below, I follow a current all the way to the ocean. Below me, a beautiful yet desolate crystal garden coats giant clam shells, mutant two-head shark skeletons, and sunken ships.

I wonder if the crystals are affecting the lady-matons' sensors because I easily evade underwater patrolling Dahomeys, Gladyses gathering crystal samples, and more Saraswatis in seeming prayer around subaqueous oxygenators. Whatever the case, I am thankful and relieved to reach my former oceanic base—what's left of it.

From beneath the waves, I gaze up at the broken shell of my

once glorious cubic laboratory. Most of the supports remain, jagged ends stabbing out of the water and dotted with barnacle-like crystalline growths; the beams still hold aloft the frame of my giant clock window. It's difficult to not give in to a bevy of emotions, but I have no time for sentiment.

I turn my gaze downward, and my monocle projects a pulsating search beam. The readings come back a mess—the crystals are absolutely affecting sensors. It's almost impossible to compensate for their refracting effect, but finally, I manage to make out the distinctive outline of what looks like a treasure chest.

I smash the crystal around it to expose the lid and handles, and I try to pull the container free. It won't budge. With a heavy sigh, I say, "*Patentibus.*"

The lid obeys, popping back. Water fills it, and I grimace as the pages of my memoir drift out. They float upward. I briefly catch the words, *The Rules of Time Travel*, before they're carried away by the current. I gaze at the bottom of the trunk, reach in, and remove an intricate key with the design of a spider in a web. It looks archaic but is the highest of tech.

I place it against my chest; the device sticks like a magnetic broach.

Unum ad alterum, I think. One down, one to go.

My boots propel me toward what's left of my underwater library. It's flooded but, suspended from what's left of the base above, not yet overgrown with crystals. Water seems to slow the formation of crystals, but given time, this will all surely be hard as rock.

I pass through a broken window pane, cut the propulsion from my boot thrusters, and sink to the floor. Fighting a wave of nostalgia, I walk through the remains of my collection. Gathered from years of plunder, it's now broken, scattered, and dotted with bits of glowing gems.

I stop next to the katana that can cut through anything, a trophy for what I thought was my greatest victory, but which I now see was the beginning of my end. I bend to the floor, pick up the weapon in its sheathe, and, without further sentiment, my boots propel me over to my convertible.

I pop the trunk, place the katana inside, and close the compartment.

"I'll see you soon," I assure the weapon. "Be ready."

I hover next to the deep-sea diver in the driver's seat, yank him out, and toss him aside.

His form floats amidst the detritus of my life then sinks; its arms settle to either side of my vintage typewriter somehow still atop my golden cog desk; the portcullis on his helmet hits the keys as if he's fallen asleep from a long night's work. If only I, too, could rest. Instead, I take his place in the car, press a few buttons on the dashboard, and get out. The vehicle's tires retract, coverings form over them, and the vehicle gently lifts.

I salute the conveyance. "May your journey be unhindered by lady-matons."

The convertible flashes its lights in response then moves gently into a current that should take it in low-power stealth mode to its destination.

I look about my shattered library and stare at the fallen bones of a T-Rex as if it can give me courage for my next, more dangerous task.

HOURS LATER, after dodging more oceanic Dahomey patrols, I reach an underwater intake pipe sticking out of a ridge covered in glittering gems. I gaze into the enormous duct's black maw. My skin prickles.

I can do this. I must *do this!*

I put the suit on auto, close my eyes, and propel toward the pipe.

It suctions me in, buffets me until I reach the terminus, then blasts me out a maintenance cover. I land on my hands and knees, gasping as a gush of water drops around me.

Distracting music inside my suit helps me get my hyperventilating under control. "♪♪ I'm still standing ..."

I get to my feet and take in the grimy hall. Condensation plops on my shoulder from pipes running the length of the ceiling. When this was my factory, everything was pristine. Clearly, Mairī Lin has other priorities. One more reason for why she is unworthy and why I must be the final victor.

I put the cover back over the watermain, press a hidden panel that causes a secret door to open in the wall, and enter a series of narrow passageways. The villain who built this place before I annexed it was both eccentric and paranoid. It was a fluke I ever discovered these cleverly cloaked corridors.

I move hastily through the pathways until I pass a one-way view panel overlooking the facility's generator room.

Bald purple Dahomeys bark orders and unleash sizzling plasma whips at the robots I designed. They whimper and wobble on misaligned uni-wheels, bulbous bodies covered in dents and scorch marks. They shovel fuel pellets into the flames of an enormous, blistering furnace, shaking as they fitfully draw power from their overused and undercharged energy cells. They were built for menial tasks, but not like this and *not* for her.

You will pay for this insult, Mairī Lin Monroe.

I lift my chin, nurse the sentiment in my mind, and stealthily travel through the hidden passageways until I reach a dusty backup control center. Dozens of monitors are set in a semi-circular wall before a wonderfully anachronistic-looking control panel.

"*Dominus imperium,*" I murmur, fighting back a tear.

Despite my predicament, I feel a spark of elusive joy as I set to flicking switches. The board powers up. It's networked in such a way that Mairī Lin and her stupid Gladys persona should not detect the activation.

In fact, this iso-station is designed for exactly this type of hostile takeover. Mairī Lin's overrun my factory, but she's not the first mad genius to try such a move. She is among the few to pull it off and the only one to do so on an all-encompassing scale—for now.

Inspired by the hidden corridors within this facility, I've constructed data backdoors into the hardware that runs my (her) vast industrial complex, on planet and in orbit. With my headquarters and tactical bases destroyed, I can only access them from here of all places—an assembly plant!

Despite my OCD over-planning for every imaginable scenario, I never believed I would need my emergency reclamation apparatus on such a system-wide level—and there is a risk in using it. I'm in the belly of the beast. It's taken every ounce of courage I didn't know I had to come here. It's a testament to my desperation. Because if I'm wrong, if Mairī Lin detects me, I'm done for.

Please, let this work.

From around my neck, I take the key with the spider in the web and insert it into a port. I pause for a moment to appreciate the momentousness of this critical juncture in history.

Or is it herstory? I wonder.

"*Omnibus aut nihil*," I murmur—all or nothing—and I jerk the key clockwise.

Mechanisms turn within; needle gauges flutter, lights flash, and the wall of monitors flare to life as the spiderweb key uploads the malware that is central to my plan to reclaim all that she has taken from me. I watch the progress bar with growing excitement until it blinks the *magicae* words.

UPLOAD COMPLETE.

I don't cry *triumphi* because this is not enough to get me across the finish line. *Tempus duo*—Phase 2—is far more dangerous.

I remove the key. As soon as I do, the monitors flicker and show me images from around the globe. My jaw lowers in horror as I gaze at feeds of my (her) facilities working at a capacity I never achieved, churning out lady-matons by the hundreds of thousands.

Excrementi! I swear.

I knew her output went beyond my most glorious doomsday machinations—but seeing it is something else. The moment a new unit steps out of a printer, be she Dahomey, Saraswati, or Gladys, she immediately sets to work expanding the industrial machine complex to build more of herself.

She/they are multiplying at an exponential rate.

Sweat drips down my back, and I wonder, even with my malware, am I too late?

"No," I assure myself, bolstering my resolve and restraining a diabolical laugh. "My plan is perfect. She may have numbers on her side, but I have something better. Me."

But am I enough?

In the time it's taken me to break into the plant and insert my hijacking gram into the infrastructure network, Mairī Lin and her alters have multiplied at such a rate, they've infested almost every measure of space in the facility. I barely make it to an effluent pipe undetected to make my escape.

My return to my comic book lair is equally harrowing. The sensor refracting crystals can only help me so much. I barely elude the growing volume of underwater Dahomeys armed with harpoons and aerial models brandishing armor-piercing rifles with laser scopes. Despite the odds, I make it back to the comic book store undetected.

When the sensor-shielded door closes behind me, I throw my sweaty arms around dummy Genetrix and hug her tight. It takes fully 10 minutes for my ragged breath to slow. I pull away and gaze into her unflinching eyes.

"I know," I nod at her unspoken words. "They'll soon be able to patrol every measure of the planet. I can't stay here. It isn't safe. It's time, isn't it?"

Genetrix and I gaze at a cone of luminescence from an artfully angled bulb. The beam creates a dramatic halo around my new armor, still hidden under a shiny cape and encircled by twinkling string lights.

I grip the satiny fabric.

"*Nunc futuri*," I declare. I jerk the covering and flick it aside.

"Behold!" I say to an imaginary audience. "The future is now."

It's a bold proclamation. Seeing the fruits of my covert labor makes me believe it. My new armor is a cornucopia of unnecessary geometric shapes layered on top of each other, more elaborate than any of my past battle suits. I disrobe from the barebones prototype and toss it into a corner like a pile of dirty clothes; I'm done with stealth.

I put a hand on dummy Genetrix's back.

"Mairī Lin Monroe will rue the day she crossed paths with me."

I snap my fingers; the armor floats off the counter, stands before me, and its intricate folds open. I step into it, and the suit click-click-clicks shut around my frame.

I salute the dummy.

"When next we meet, Genetrix, you'll be bleeping like your old self."

I chuckle at her silent response. "Oh, you; we have our squabbles, but you do make me laugh."

OUTSIDE MY COMIC BOOK LAIR, I evade fly-by patrols, break through the layer of crystal crusting over Restitution River, and navigate underwater past more Dahomeys, toward my end game.

I ride a sweeping current that takes me over the remains of my old ocean base, through a sunken city I once hoped to reclaim and name Atlantis, all the way to a flooded cavern that the Dahomeys have not discovered (or don't care about).

Waiting for me, safely submerged, is my convertible. It bobs in low-power mode. Bits of crystal stick to it. I open the trunk and remove Caitlin's katana. I pull the blade a measure from its scabbard. The unbreakable metal glints.

"No more encores," I say. "It's time for the finale."

I shove the blade back into its sheath, float over and into the convertible's flooded driver's seat, and strap on the safety belt. At a touch, the vehicle hums and vibrates to life.

"Fire," I command.

The convertible's headlights retract, and they launch a pair of torpedoes. I watch the bubbly wake they create, grip the steering wheel, and growl as the missiles explode against the crystal layer above. My foot rams the accelerator, the convertible blasts through the opening, out of the water, and into the air.

Glittery water drains out of the car and flies behind me, forming a misty rainbow as the crystal particulates refract the light from the blazing sun above. Of course, my armored self doesn't need the vehicle to transport me from point A to B. No, the purpose of my conveyance is to dazzle and distract.

As a lone cloud moves slowly into place, my hoverconvertible rockets above what was once a bay. Now, it's covered in a thick layer of glittering orange citrine. Behind me, an enormous jade bridge spans from nowhere to once was.

I race across the bay's smooth surface, toward the shore of the city that was to be my global capital until Mairī Lin decisively made it her own.

Ahead, amethyst crags rise on the outskirts of a vast crystal desert that surrounds Mairī Lin's seat of power. In the sky above, hundreds of purple Dahomeys come together.

"So, you did survive," they snort. Their chorus of voices washes over me. They pull blasters and laser swords from their hips. I don't give them a chance to use them.

"Magnet-o-thon, activate!" I shout.

A compartment on my armor's shoulder pops open, hisses air, and releases a floating red globe. It bobs at my side for a moment before firing into the midst of the Dahomeys diving toward me. Their quasi-eyes blink languidly in surprise.

Please work please work please …

The device activates, glowing like a sun, and the throng of Dahomeys is immediately pulled into it, their bodies crushing against each other. In seconds, they form a massive purple ball of mangled, twitching limbs and contorted faces that drops and slams into the crystalized bay.

I wish I'd had the time and material to make more magnet-o-thons—until the polarized sphere of spasming body parts pulls the car toward it.

Damnare!

I press the turbo boost, grit my teeth, and force the steering wheel back on course.

I reach what was once a port. Barges and other maritime vessels tilt at awkward angles amidst jutting columns of crystal. Above a dock, a rusted sign has been painted over in green and decaled with the words:

Welcome to MEGALOPOLIS

I recognize the font.

The sign's been kept free of crystals. Is that for my benefit? Is Mairī Lin expecting me or simply hoping I'd come? It matters not. Either way, she'll regret her hubris.

What seems a lifetime ago, our battle leveled the city that once stood here; in its place, diamond towers now reach for the sun. Giant jewels surround obsidian pyramids, tiger's eye domes, and bloodstone spirals. Three sky-scraping obelisks rise in the city's center, each in a different color—green, orange, and purple. They form a triangle around an even taller tower that glitters fuchsia-pink. Shiny, sweeping bridges connect the four constructs.

Fools might consider this "Megalopolis" an architectural marvel, but I know garbage urban planning when I see it.

My suit's built-in binoculars reveal robots of my design hovering around the towers, some holding buckets, others scrubbing the glittering surface with brushes and mops.

She could've given them power washers, but no. She wants it to be as menial as possible. She can have her petty moment because soon, the victory of all victories shall be mine.

My foot pushes the accelerator; wind whips around my armored form. The single cloud in the sky is almost in place.

"Begin countdown," I say. Inside my helm, a hologram of my lost timepiece starts running.

"Intruder alert, intruder alert!" my former robots intone in sing-song voices from around the towers. Gone are their bleeps and blops. My fingers tense on the wheel.

What has that malicious monster done to their vocal programming?

It's one more thing to bind her death warrant.

My binoculars enlarge the sight of Mairī Lin as she flies to the top of one of the obelisk bridges; a Gladys, a Saraswati, and a Dahomey land at her side.

"Finally," my audio attuners catch the Dahomey saying in the distance, "I can kill him."

We'll see who kills who, I think. I glance at the hologram counting down inside my helm.

"Activate malware," I bark.

My viral programming kicks in, and the robots built in my design turn their heads to the sky; their voice boxes blare a song I listened to over and over as I calculatingly probed Mairī Lin's movie playlist to discern exploitable weaknesses.

"♪♪Melancholy baby ..." my bots play from an audiograph pinned to a digital board Mairī Lin labeled as Happy-Sad Favorites. When it gets to the part about clouds and silver linings, I realize I'm singing along—not because I like it, I assure myself, but because I *am* the cloud *and* the silver lining all in one—as she will see.

The Dahomey on the bridge grabs the singing robot nearest to her, rips out its audio box, and crushes the device in her palm. The apparatus squawks and goes silent, but the rest of my bots keep playing the warbling tune.

"He's jacked into the robots," green, spectacled Gladys cries.

I couldn't hijack the lady-matons—they house a super genius, after all—but my bots are *my* bots.

"Override him!" Dahomey orders as if she were the primary.

"I'm trying!" Gladys says.

"Do I have to do everything myself?" Dahomey demands. She draws the pistol magnetically clamped to her hip. In the time it takes me to take a single breath, she shoots a dozen of my robots through their central processors, blowing their gears out the backs of their transparent heads. Clang! Rattle! Crash! In quick succession, they drop and go silent. The melody they're projecting gets quieter with each one that falls.

"Stop it!" Mairī Lin cries, holding up her hand imperiously.

The Dahomey's outline of a mouth gnashes.

"Let me go!" she growls, aiming her pistol at another of my bots. I wait for it to fall victim to her rage—a pawn sacrificed in this deadly game of chess—but the bot remains intact, singing louder. It would seem Dahomey is no longer able to pull the trigger —try as she might—as something unseen restrains her quivering finger.

"Help me!" Dahomey says to Saraswati.

The orange lady-maton looks from her purple sister-self to Mairī Lin then back. Saras shrugs. "I love this song."

Exactly, I think. My plan goes better than expected as half a dozen Saraswatis fly onto the bridge. Their sweet, melodious voices join in, creating a harmonious counterpoint to the baritone of my bots. The orange lady-matons begin dancing in sync in a style I recognize from the screenings contained in a streaming playlist Mairī Lin's labeled "Bollywood."

They're going to love what I have planned next.

"Stop it!" the Gladys says, grabbing the nearest Saraswati. She hooks her multi-arms about Gladys' waist, hand, head, and hip, dragging her through a series of thumkas and hastas. It almost looks fun. I may even rewatch a few of Mairī Lin's (and Saras') Bollywood "favs"—after I kill them.

"Dance is a poem," Saraswati explains, as if this logic can bring the intellectual Gladys on side.

"It's a trick," the green lady-maton insists.

"We used to love poetry; don't you remember?" the Saraswatis sigh in unison. "Now, we don't have to merely read it. We can *move* it!"

"We're smarter than this," the Gladys begs, stumbling and trying to disentangle herself.

"Sometimes the dumb thing is the smart thing," Mairī Lin replies, jumping to the front of what's turned into a group choreographed routine. The Saras follow their pink primary's lead.

"That makes no sense," the Gladys insists.

"Agreed," Dahomey says.

The Saraswatis hesitate, pause in their dance, then echo with a sigh, "Agreed."

Mairī Lin pirouettes to face her alters.

"Are you all ganging up on me?" Mairī Lin asks.

"Yes," they reply as one.

No! I rage. I need to keep her distracted. If she detects what I'm really up to …

"Release the package!" I order.

A small hot-air balloon with propellers descends from its hiding place in the cloud I've maneuvered into position. A metal claw on the dirigible's underside opens, releasing a box gift wrapped in shiny orange, purple, and green, and tied with a pink bow. A parachute unfurls, and the gift floats downward. Dahomey wrenches herself free of whatever's been holding her back and aims her pistol at the box.

"Wait," Mairī Lin says. "Sensors aren't picking up any threats."

"He *is* the threat!" Dahomey replies.

I need more time.

"Next track!" I shout.

'Melancholy Baby' fades, and up come the lyrics, "🎵 material girl…"

The outline of Mairī Lin's eyes widens. The Saraswatis look tortured.

"This is one of our favorites!" they say.

Yes, I think, driving faster across the glittering expanse surrounding her city. *I know.*

"Saraswati, Gladys, aren't you just dying to see what's inside the box?" Mairī Lin asks. "Creatively and intellectually?"

They hesitate, look at each other, nod in agreement, and come to stand next to Mairī Lin.

"Idiots!" Dahomey rages.

Veritas, I think gleefully.

The gift lands in the center of the lady-matons.

Mairī Lin rips away the wrapping and jerks off the lid. Her etched mouth grins as she holds up a dark suit and a monocle. "Gladys, this will fit you perfectly! And look here," Mairī Lin pulls out a pink dress and a diamond necklace, "for you, Saraswati. And for Dahomey, a skin-tight studded black PVC unitard with a cone-bra!" Dahomey grudgingly accepts the garment from Mairī Lin. "And for me …"

Mairī Lin holds up a cleavage-revealing white dress.

"It's just like in the screening!" she coos. "Put them on! Put them on!"

A Saraswati and the Gladys do. The Dahomey hesitates, then, as if forcing herself, she rips her garment down the middle and throws the severed cone-bra over the bridge.

"Bazooka," she barks. One of my still singing robots hands her the weapon. She accepts it, rips out the robot's audio box, and turns the weapon toward me.

"No!" Mairī Lin insists. She stumbles, half in her dress, and shoves the bazooka as Dahomey fires. The ballistic leaves a smoke trail as it flies through the air and explodes to my left. The force rocks the convertible. I grit my teeth, jerk the steering wheel to compensate, and keep from flipping over.

Almost there, I think.

"Activate attack pattern alpha," I say.

The entire city—her so-called Megalopolis—shakes and quakes as if at the epicenter of a geo-seismic or thermonuclear event. The monolithic towers and connecting bridges tremble violently, knocking Mairī Lin and the other lady-matons off our feet.

My recently co-opted robots haven't had much time since I infiltrated my (Mairī Lin's) factory, but they are efficient. Giant decorative orbs, cubes, and cylinders open like budding flowers, revealing massive steam-powered machines of churning gears, pistons, levers, and random propellers.

A line of octagonal prisms transforms into vertical pressure release conduits, whistling steam at their ends; levers burst out of hidden recesses in roads paved with polished hematite; five of my bots combine to transform into a giant, cog-driven clock with pumping copper pistons. Within Mairī Lin's crystalline hell, I've created a retro-futuristic stage for the greatest show this world will ever see.

In a blink, I spot a dozen flaws, but given how little time my recently co-opted bots had, and without Genetrix to stage manage, I grudgingly admit, they've done well. I glance at the holographic chronometer counting down inside my helm. Imperfect or not, this just has to distract Mairī Lin and her system for a little bit longer.

My bots grab the levers, pulling them one way, then pushing them the other, as if this were necessary for keeping some expansive industrial complex running. Mairī Lin covers her mouth, takes it in, then claps.

Good, I think. She recognizes and is mesmerized by the montage I've created, an ode to the screening that inspired the name Megalopolis and one of the videographs by the material girl songstress.

I stand in the hovercar and point Caitlin's katana before me; a circular energy pod glows on my armored chest; a trio of cylinders pop out from hidden recesses on the back; they blast me out of the vehicle and into the set I've created within the crystal metropolis. Dahomey reloads her bazooka and aims it at me.

"Now!" I cry before she can fire.

The music changes; the robots built in my factory blare, "♪♪ Express yourself!"

"Freeze!" Mairī Lin orders the Dahomey. The purple robot once more struggles to pull the trigger, unable to move a mechanized muscle.

"He's playing you!" Dahomey growls.

"But isn't it the most interesting thing that's happened to us in forever?" Mairī Lin replies. "It's been so boring without him."

"My job is to keep us all safe!" Dahomey growls. "*Not* entertained."

"But I *need* variety," Mairī Lin insists. "Safety is death."

I land at the base of the four towers amidst my robots operating the levers of my steam factory set. I clap my hands overhead; they abandon their workstations and fall in line behind me. Mairī Lin pulls the straps of her dress atop her shoulders and leans over the bridge rail to watch me.

With the bots from my factory acting as backup, my preprogrammed armor compensates for my lack of rhythm and my bum leg. I lead the dance I've stolen from the videograph made to accompany this song. That video is populated by muscled pretty boys speckled with soot. I'm nothing like that. I'm something better. As if to prove it, I've thrown in a few of Mairī Lin's Bollywood moves and matching harmonics, "mashing up" the dichotomous yet oddly congruent beats.

"Yass!" Mairī Lin cries.

I smile. She gets it—and it shall be her doom.

"You have to let me destroy his bots!" Dahomey insists.

"Not yet," Mairī Lin says; her pink chrome eyes are wide with excitement. "It's too wonderful!"

The labradorite, pyrite, and quartz that comprise the city's bedrock throb from the song. The vibrations ripple up the towers and outward, beyond Megalopolis, washing over the amethyst encrusted dock, sea ships, and bay to the west and the crescent-shaped mountain range to the east, north, and south. It's once snowy peaks glitter with palpitating diamonds. My sensors confirm the vibrations are reaching further still, to every corner of the globe, moving downward just as quickly, to the earth's very core.

In moments, the entire planet quivers in time to the song.

"What's happening?" Dahomey demands of Gladys.

The song builds to a crescendo. The crystals shake more intensely. Gladys screams, grips her temples, and drops to her knees.

"He's hacked into other systems!" Gladys warns.

"Which systems?" Dahomey demands.

"Scanning," Gladys pants.

"We have to put a stop to this," the frozen Dahomey growls at the Saraswatis.

Two of the orange lady-matons kneel next to the suffering Gladys.

"Agreed," the Saraswatis nod.

They close their eyes in concentration, hands forming the shakata mudra, ring finger and thumb pressed together. They surround Mairī Lin like angry villagers from bygone days about to stone a thief among them, and they intone, "Exorcise the demon."

"Rude!" Mairī Lin says, stumbling and grabbing the handrail as if thrown off balance. The demon they speak of is her controlling presence within their shared network.

Dahomey's frozen form thaws. She fires the bazooka. The projectile blasts toward me. One of my bots flies kamikaze into the missile and explodes in the air.

"Even better," Dahomey says to me from above. "I'll enjoy tearing you apart with my bare hands."

She jumps off the bridge and cracks the vibrating crystal where she lands, a few short measures from me.

I need 30 more seconds. I have scads more songs, but I don't think that's going to distract them any longer.

"Without the heart," I lift Caitlin's katana and shout, "there can be no understanding between the hand and the mind!"

Do my stolen words from the screening that inspired the name Megalopolis give Mairī Lin strength? I'd say so. She pushes past the Saraswatis, flips over the railing, and softly alights next to Dahomey. The pink primary grasps the purple warrior's biceps with what appears to be a feather touch, yet the muscled, domineering lady-maton can't break free.

"Let go of me!" she insists. Mairī Lin is back where I need her —in control.

On the bridge above, green Gladys struggles to her feet. "You have to help Dahomey," Gladys says to her orange sister-selves.

The Saraswatis nod. They assume an unconventional battle configuration, forming various gestures with their quadruplet of hands—interlaced fingers with palms facing the chest and thumbs pointing up to the sky; left knuckles to heart with right palm on top; fingers laced together, index finger pointing out.

Surely the Saraswatis don't need to make these gestures to focus their psyches as they vie to wrest control from Mairī Lin, but I do like the way they look. Perhaps I'll steal them when I rewind and add them to my showmanship repertoire. Such are my thoughts— until my defensive sensors identify and create a holo list of the mudras her hands are forming—Vajrapradama, Ganesh, and Kali. Unshakable. Remover of Obstacles. Destruction.

Next to each is a threat level assessment—UNKNOWN.

And suggested countermeasure—UNKNOWN.

The Saraswatis chant; in response, Dahomey's muscles swell, and she breaks free of Mairī Lin's grip.

"Ow!" the petite pink simulacrum says, her blond hair bobbing.

Dahomey ignores her, focusing solely on me.

"You're dead," she says. All around me, crystal formations open, and out step hundreds of purple lady-matons.

Just a few more seconds, I think. The holo chronometer in my helm speeds toward zero.

"You're too late," I say, pointing the katana skyward.

They look upward. Mairī Lin presses her hand to her heaving chest.

"*Nunc futuri,*" I murmur.

My timer dings, the song ends, and the crystals vibrate more wildly. My robots begin projecting a new song—'O Fortuna' from the opera *Carmina Burana*.

A blinding burst of energy blasts down from *my* death ray on the moon. My robots aren't the only tech I've reclaimed. According to my sensors, the beam explodes into the center of the city and successfully penetrates through to the crystalline figure at the heart of the crystals' growth.

I activate my see-through vision to watch the beam shove a pulsing glow into the figure of a crystalline woman locked in a silent scream. The voiceless howl of Mairī Lin's frenemy distorts into a melting horror mask as her form heats up and turns molten. She cycles through a variety of glowing hues, turns onyx black, and explodes into shards.

"Tourmaline!" Mairī Lin cries, clearly seeing what I'm seeing using see-through vision of her own.

Just as the vibrations spread through the crystals, so too does the beam.

All around us, crystals glow a bevy of oscillating colors, the shifting spectrum altering their lattice matrix on a quantum level. The colors fade, replaced by light-absorbing black. They shake violently and shatter; shards break against my armor.

Onward, the beam spreads, snaking up the quartet of obelisks dominating Megalopolis, out into the diamond tips of the surrounding crescent-shaped mountain range, and toward the docks and boats trapped in a crystal grave that begins flashing a multitude of colors

The light in them shrinks into onyx black, the crystals shake more violently, and erupt into dust. The four monoliths in the city's center crumble, followed by everything around them. A thick cloud of sparkling dust billows outward, knocking me, Mairī Lin, and her lady-matons off their feet.

Laughing feverishly, I watch the modified death ray continue its viral journey through the parasitic crystals penetrating the globe.

More crystals flash, turn black, and pop.

All over the world, the cage that's kept me from time-traveling shatters on a sub-atomic level.

I spread my arms wide, and cry, "*Triumphi!*"

Part III

Chapter 14

A layer of twinkling soot covers everything, surrounding me in a great ebony desert. My bots rise out of the ashes. I gaze at my blackened form in the reflection of Caitlin's blade. Perhaps my moniker in my next timeline should be Phoenix. The cadre of Saraswatis from the now-dissolved tower bridge lands along with the green Gladys. Gladys crumples to her knees. Her shoulders heave as she scoops a handful of the black dust, letting it sift through her fingers.

"It's gone; all gone!" she cries.

"We can rebuild," the Saraswatis assure her.

"With what?" Gladys demands. She grabs another handful of black sand and shakes it in her fist. "This is useless."

"There are other planets," the Saraswatis say.

I gaze skyward. Intergalactic colonization? Now that is an idea worth stealing. Who knows what resources lie amongst the stars!

"What about our organic body?" Gladys asks. "It can't survive that kind of journey."

I'd almost forgotten. Now that Mairī Lin's quantum stabilizing crystals have been dealt with, it's time to eliminate her bio form.

She must be nearby—possibly buried and choking on what's left of her crystals, but I have to be sure.

"Begin enemy detection sequence M-L-M," I command.

"Searching, searching," my robots intone as their sensors seek her life signs. At my earliest opportunity, I will revert them to bleeps and bloops.

"Failure, failure," they report. "No life signs detected."

"You can't hide forever, not from me," I declare, "for I am Dr. BetterThanYou. I had hoped to gloat over you in this timeline, but I shall settle for doing so in the next."

I tilt my chin imperiously and mentally turn the time travel key in my mind, palm poised above the internal activation switch—until a metallic hand thrusts up from the glittering black powder at my feet.

Purple fingers crush the armor around my ankle and smash my body face-first into the top of a smokestack leftover from my performance and poking out from the black desert. In a flash of purple, a Dahomey bursts out of the ash and is on top of me, punching my helm repeatedly with terrifying speed and force. I try to swing Caitlin's blade; Dahomey smacks it from my hand then returns to pummeling me. My inertial dampeners can't keep up with the relentless blows, smacking my head against the inside of my protective helm.

I try to time jump, but the ringing in my skull is too much.

"You're not going anywhere," the spectacle-wearing Gladys explains. She stands, fists clenched and body shaking. She rips off the black lady-suit I gave her. "I deduced which regions of your brain control your temporal abilities. Dahomey's targeting them."

The purple lady-maton continues to pummel me. I try to activate my power; the quantum-stabilizing crystals are gone, but with my head injury, I almost pass out.

I fire ember energy from my wrist blaster, and a black hole erupts behind the Dahomey, sucking her into its crushing depths. The black hole disappears.

All around, purple lady-matons rise from the ash; it dusts their shoulders and bare scalps.

I point the weapon at a pair of purple lady-matons closing in with energy tomahawks crackling from their batons. I'm about to fire, but the intellectual Gladys hisses, jumps, and stabs my blaster with a computer pen. My blackhole generator sparks, creates a mini black maw that rips the weapon and e-pen into itself, and the suctioning gravity well vanishes a second later.

I unclasp a triangle from my hip and stick it between Gladys' green breasts. A cyclone erupts around her, spins her shrieking frame, and tears her apart.

A Dahomey tackles me, pinning my arms and legs to the ground. Shiny discs fly off my armor, hovering and spinning in the air as they power up their lasers, ready to blast her. The army of purple lady-matons shoots the saucers like they're target practice.

"Robots!" I shout. "Protect me!"

The bots made in my factory execute the surrounding Dahomeys in the backs of their heads, then aim their weapons at the Dahomey holding me against the ground. The black sands shift, forming sinkholes from which green Gladyses emerge.

"Malware neutralized," they declare.

My smile fades.

"*Excremente*," I swear.

Dahomey's lips twitch a rare smile. "Activate self-destruct!"

All around, my reclaimed bots blow to pieces.

I have to get out of here. The trio of cylinders on my back activate. I'm about to rocket away from her, but she swiftly wraps her arms around me and crushes the jets in a bear hug. They sputter, burp, and go dark.

My boot blasters activate, getting me a measure above her—until she grabs my ankle and jerks me down. She tears the round battery packet from my chest, looking like she'll go for my heart next. My boots go dead; I drop to ground, jamming my spine as my butt hits a dense, black rock.

"I promised to protect Mairī Lin from people like you, users and fake romantics," the purple lady-maton says, towering over me, "and I'm going to even if I have to put her in a cage to do it!"

The Dahomey rips off my helmet, leaving my bruised head wholly exposed. I pant. My arms fall limp. Dahomey's purple fingers curl into a fist.

I'm dead I'm—

Dahomey's head explodes. Blue goo flies everywhere; her body shudders, releases me, and topples over. Behind her stands pink Mairī Lin, white dress dusted with ash, a smoking blaster in hand.

The remaining purple lady-matons turn on her. Faster than my eye can follow, Mairī Lin blasts them too. They crumple, forming a battlefield of fallen, headless, purple shells.

I take a gasping, desperate breath.

"You ... you saved me," I say.

"I've doomed us both," she says, shaking her head sadly, making her blond hair bob. "I've just declared war—on myself."

Her words make no sense. If she's trying to confuse me, it's working. I step, and my bum knee buckles. I fall to all fours.

Mairī Lin kneels next to me and cups my cheeks. I brace myself for her to crush my skull.

She presses her metal lips to mine. They move as much as they're able.

Is she kissing me?

I feel a strange stirring, like a heated eel is curiously exploring my insides. Is she transferring energy from her power core into me through our physical contact? She pulls away; an echo of her warmth remains.

"I think this was our best date yet," she says.

"Date?" I ask.

"You even made me a playlist," she thrills.

"I did?" I ask.

"Who would have guessed you were such a romantic," she says.

"This *wasn't* romantic," I insist. It hurts to breathe; I'm pretty sure my ankle's broken, but her mockery is worse than the physical pain; I *won't* have her diminishing my grand plan like this—especially since I won; I think. "It was a trick, and you fell for it."

"That's what romance is," she explains patiently. "A trick we play on others and ourselves. But, from time to time, it leads to something more, to something real."

More Gladyses emerge from where they were buried, joined by orange Saras. They tremble as they stare at the Dahomey headless torsos littering the sooty ground.

"What have you done?" they demand.

They gaze into the distance; a purple storm is rumbling toward us in the windless air. The weather system gets closer impossibly fast. My eyes widen. Those aren't clouds. It's Dahomeys. There must be hundreds of thousands of them, converging from all over the globe. Streaks of orange and green come from the opposite horizon as an armada of Gladyses and Saras abandon their far-flung posts.

The different colored lady-matons arrive simultaneously. Some of the Gladyses and Saras land, others stay in the air; all of them use their bodies to form a protective wall around Mairī Lin, one that happens to enclose me as well.

"Don't!" the green and orange lady-matons beg of their purple sister-self. "She's our primary!"

"Not for long," the Dahomeys reply, shoving the weaker models aside and closing in like a swarm of angry hornets.

"Stop!" Mairī Lin shouts, holding her hand up, palm out. The Dahomeys slow but don't halt.

The Saras place their pointing fingers together, thumbs up, and begin to chant.

"Don't you dare try to quiet my mind!" the Dahomeys yell; each grabs the nearest Saras, rips its head off, and tosses the torso aside. The Gladyses cover their mouths in shock.

The Dahomeys on the ground gain step by step; the ones in the air, push by push.

"You chose *him* over us?" the purples demand of Mairī Lin.

Their unified voice is deafening. "After all we've done for you? And for what? A pretty dress and a dance routine?"

"We need him!" Mairī Lin shouts back.

Need me? What? Why?

"We don't need anybody but ourselves," the closest Dahomey replies.

"Everybody needs somebody," Mairī Lin pleads.

The surviving Saras nod. "He shares our taste in music. He's creative. And brilliant."

Their orange faces turn to the Gladyses.

"His technology's all stolen," the green lady-matons say.

"But look what he's done with it," Mairī Lin says.

"It's not … unimpressive," the nearest Gladys concedes. "And he is a time traveler." She looks at me. "I still think about your memoirs."

Really?

"You must have so many more stories to share," Mairī Lin says to me.

"Indeed, he must," a Gladys sighs, coming to stand at Mairī Lin's right; a Saras joins on her left. All three of them raise a hand toward the lead Dahomey.

The purple lady-matons freeze where they float or stand. Mairī Lin's pink face turns to me. "We can't hold them for long. They're too angry."

She helps me to my feet. I wince, but as long as I keep my weight on my other leg, I can stand.

"You have to go." She slaps a round device onto the shoulder of my battered suit. The device whirls and powers up the anti-grav packs in my boots.

"What are you—"

She kisses me again with her warm metal lips; she pulls away, and my boots blast me into the air. I screech in surprise.

She waves at me from below. "Goodbye, my Timematician."

Her words stick in my ears when I should be thinking about

anything but. Without my helmet, I can't control where I'm going. I zig-zag amidst the airborne Dahomeys in a twirling route, pin-balling against some, evading others by chance. They're stuck in place, but a few catch hold of me, ripping off pieces of my armor as I tear free. One Dahomey manages a precision punch to the device Mairī Lin pinned to my chest. The battery cracks and sputters.

I drop from the air; my arms flail amidst reaching purple hands. *I'm dead I'm dead I'm …*

I break free of their mass, fall dozens of measures, and crash into the ground. Black dust poofs around me.

I grunt. I have just enough armor left to survive the impact—if barely. I don't think the fall's broken anything. In front of me is my hovercar, the one I rode in on full of plans for redemption.

I touch my lips where Mairī Lin's met mine.

"I'm coming for you!" the Dahomeys cry. Mairī Lin still holds them, but for how long?

I crawl to the car, yank the door open, and struggle in. I drive away as fast as I can, the car skimming over black ash. The Dahomeys squirm but are unable to break free of Mairī Lin's control. One of the purple lady-matons rips her own arm off and throws it at me so hard it smashes into the convertible's dashboard. The vehicle's front dips, hits the ground, and I barely get it back up and under control.

I pull the arm free; purple fingers try to grab me; I throw the limb overboard.

The damaged convertible whines and sputters, pulling to the left, but I manage to keep it on course. To my relief, there's no sign of pursuit.

I make it safely back to the broken city battered by a once perpetual electrical storm that's now almost dissipated. I can only postulate that my death beams destabilized it. The damaged car rattles as I power it down; instead of gently setting itself on the ground, it drops like a brick, hitting hard and jarring my neck.

I don't think I'll be driving it again in this timeline. I pat it mournfully. "You served with honor, good stead. You deserve a hero's burial, but alas, the battle is not yet won."

I conceal the car under a cloaking tarp that makes it blend with the black dust all around. While the vehicle is dead, I survive and am very much in pain.

Inside my comic book lair, I hammer a screwdriver into my beaten armor to pry off the pieces. When I get to my broken ankle, I look to dummy Genetrix for encouragement.

"I'm brave I'm brave I'm …"

I pound the screwdriver and yank, howling and almost passing out from the pain.

I activate the cellular regenerator from the first aid kit, pass the wand over my broken joint and bruised throat, wincing as the device speeds the healing. The regenerator helps, but it can only do so much.

I pass the healing wand around my battered head and concussed brain, realizing now that's where I should've started. The pounding in my temples doesn't disappear, but it dims—enough, I hope.

I look at the chronometer on the computer screen of my makeshift control panel, assembled with dated and salvaged tech what seems a lifetime ago. I wish it farewell.

I'm done with this time. I'm uncertain how far back to travel, but anywhen will be better than now.

I activate the imaginary key and button in my mind, feel the lurch of my power activating, and immediately throw up. My insufficiently healed head pounds worse than before. I gaze at my computer. I've gone back eight seconds, and it felt like the quantum stream was ripping me apart.

I need more time to heal—but how much time? An hour? Days? Months? Can I survive that long against Dahomey?

I wince and grit my teeth as I limp to my substandard master control panel. I have to make sure I haven't been followed.

Before I can touch a button or pull a switch, the cracked

monitor comes to life, buzzing in and out. Mairī Lin's pink form appears on screen. She leans forward.

"Tim?" she says.

Explosions rock the room behind her, followed by laser fire. "Tim, can you hear me?" she asks. "She's coming for me. You'll be next. Our only hope is to join forces. Hurry, before it's too—"

I see a Dahomey behind Mairī Lin. The purple lady-maton is splattered with blue effluent; hers or that of her sister-selves. She raises her blaster.

"Behind you!" I shout before I can stop myself.

Dahomey fires; Mairī Lin's camera dies; my screen fills with static.

Chapter 15

My butt plonks onto a duct-taped chair.

Is she dead? I wonder. Tears bubble in my eyes. Dummy Genetrix stares at me questioningly.

"Tears of joy," I insist.

The social-ometer I installed in my suit in preparation for meeting Mairī Lin's organic body pulses $\not\in$.

"I'm not lying," I insist.

Then why is my sternum squeezing so hard it feels like my ribs are about to implode? Is it part of my injuries, or …

"Do I *like* Mairī Lin?"

My social-ometer shows the symbol $\forall$ for authenticity. Those things she said about me … Does Mairī Lin like me for real this time?

I lean over my console and type quickly, searching once more for Mairī Lin's life sign.

The word NEGATIVE flashes on my monitor.

"Think!" I shout at the mannequin. I consider its response. "Yes," I agree, "that could work."

Mairī Lin's hidden her biological signature from me, but there's a battle raging betwixt her selves. Might it not be most intense where her cellular form lies? Surely, I can detect those power fluctuations. I recalibrate my sensors.

The word LOCATED flashes on my monitor, followed by a set of coordinates.

"*Triumphi!*" I cry, hugging the mannequin dressed as Genetrix. "Well done, you beautiful plastic simulacrum!"

I punch in the coordinates, and a flashing light appears on my digital planetary map. My stomach curdles as I recognize the location.

THE ASYLUM.

It never occurred to me she would still be there, in that place.

My head turns to the shattered remains of my armor that were once an intricate assembly of over-the-top geometric shapes. Dahomey nearly crushed me alive in that thing. My gaze veers to the prototype suit that rescued me from the icy waters around my oil rig base and helped me reclaim my robots. It looks barely more than a second skin; other than a mechanized monocle and some gold etchings that were meant to be attachment points for something grander, it's purely defensive.

So what am I to do? Let the lady-matons fight amongst each other, then swoop in for the kill? That would be the most logical course of action.

I touch my lips where Mairī Lin kissed me. I didn't even care she hadn't disinfected herself. Before Genetrix can talk me out of it, I declare to her, "I will not wait here for Dahomey to come for me. Genetrix! Help me get dressed!"

Nothing happens. There is no Genetrix. I ignore the dummy's implied eye roll.

I achingly waddle to the discarded rubber-polymer suit and slide its sleeves over my arms, step into the legs, and wince as it closes around me. I holster laser pistols to my thighs and pick up the slim-fit archivist trench coat the dummy used to wear. I'm now thin enough to don it. I slide my arms through the sleeves, button it up, and catch my reflection in a cracked monitor; I look like an assassin.

Today that is what I shall be.

"You thought I was going to fly to Mairī Lin Monroe's rescue because she gave me one moment of arousal?" I say to dummy Genetrix. "Ha! I will *never* join forces with the likes of her. With Mairī Lin at war with herself, her biological body will never be more vulnerable. I'm going to kill her, once and for alls!"

Chapter 16

What my golem-esque suit lacks in panache, it makes up for in speed. I land in front of a rearing edifice. Massive rivets fasten an imposing metal sign above the open front doors.

THE ASYLUM.

The architecture reflects the institution's punitive purpose, comprised of windowless concrete walls, cantilevered isolation pods, and more barbed wire than tinsel on a holiday tree—all of it covered in a film of glittery black dust. I nervously eye a cracked polyethylene silo bleeding a cocktail of mind-castrating chemicals like sap. Pools of it bubble in dark puddles.

"*Ventri de bestia,*" I murmur.

Belly of the beast.

My spine clenches. This is where the super-geniuses who went mad would allegedly be "treated" when in truth, the only cure was a body bag. Whenever my enemies, the so-called heroes of this world, cornered me, this is where they threatened to bring me. I laughed in their faces, Caitlin's most of all. Yet alone, at night, thoughts of this place filled me with nightmares that woke me drenched in sweat.

Now, I'm here of my own volition.

It's a trap, a part of me warns. *The Dahomeys want you to come. Mairī Lin wants you to come—not to rescue her, but to make a fool of you, again. She's not helpless. She's the most dangerous foe you've ever faced. Walk away from this—while you can.*

"No," I whisper to myself.

Thick steel doors have been ripped from their hinges and lie to either side of a long black tunnel that penetrates deep into the bowels of the construct.

"*Ultimo finum ludum*," I say.

Ultimate end game.

I clench my fingers and fly into the tunnel. I wait to be tackled by seething purple lady-matons. They don't come. I stop, unimpeded, in a circular room with five corridors jutting in every direction. Crystal ash dusts the crumpled uniforms of former guards, physicians, and the incarcerated.

My hoverboots lower me to the floor; my arms and legs flex into a fighter's stance. It's so quiet, I hear water drip.

"Where are they?" I ask.

In response, my internal screen shows me the layout of the facility; cybernetic signatures are scattered throughout. Some of them flutter fitfully; others wink out permanently. I detect something else —a biological lifesign; Mairī Lin's, I presume. She's surrounded by the largest, densest cluster of cybernetic signals in the facility.

Are they waiting to ambush me? If so, I must draw them out.

"Here I am, you titillating tool!" I shout, spreading my arms wide. "Do your worst!"

My voice echoes in the cavernous institution. I brace myself for plasma fire; none comes.

"*Deodamnatus*," I swear under my breath. My systems detect a lady-maton one hallway over. I pull a photon pistol from its holster and jump around the corner, ready to fire.

An orange Saraswati sits on the floor, body propped against a wall marred by laser blasts. Two of her four arms are missing. Her body sparks at the dismembered joints and drips blue goo. Her head twitches, and she robotically intones, "System Failure. Reboot, reboot. Host reconnect in progress. Access denied."

What does that mean? I wonder.

The answer is obvious. This is a distraction, intended to confuse me into lowering my guard.

"It won't work! I'm on to you, you appalling apparatus!"

I cautiously traverse the halls of The Asylum; they are a labyrinth filled with defenses designed to neutralize the smartest and most insane of techniacs.

Set at regular intervals, roboarms attached to the walls hold what look like coronets. They're cerebral inhibitors; the insides are lined with brain screws that can drill through the skull and lobotomize within seconds.

I shoot them all, then proceed, kicking one of them aside.

Minutes later, I reach a glass-enclosed walkway leading to the wing where the most dangerous "patients" were kept. Metal tentacles dangle from the ceiling all along the bridge's length. Each tentacle is tipped with a needle capable of penetrating armor and shielding. This is how Mairī Lin intends to take me out.

I fire my photon pistols, severing the coils. They fall and writhe, spewing a cocktail of sedatives and anti-psychotics that would knock a mammoth off its feet. I step gingerly among them. A spastic coil brushes my heel. I screech and involuntarily rewind.

I feel myself stepping backward with the solidity of a fizzling hologram as my power activates. The coils reattach to the ceiling as I meet my past self, the one standing at the mouth of the walkway.

I jolt to a quantum halt and gaze at the shimmering tentacles, whole once more. My head doesn't hurt, and my nose doesn't bleed. My powers are back.

"The Timematician has returned," I smile, wondering if I should keep the title.

I could rewind further, but I'm not done with this timeline. Mairī Lin's at her most vulnerable. I certainly wouldn't want to try attacking her when The Asylum's fully staffed. I'm not letting this opportunity pass.

So I tell myself as I shoot the coils and cross the bridge.

Chapter 17

Moments later, I enter an octagonal chamber. Trap doors line the glass floors, ready to drop unruly inmates into a swirling yellow goo that I've used in one of my past timelines to subject the denizens of Jupitar City to a nightmare-wracked catatonic state.

It was hilarious.

I float over the threat, just in case.

I can time travel at the speed of thought, but if caught off guard, or I'm too slow on the draw, this or any number of remaining defensive devices could end me. I traverse corridors equipped with the most maleficent of mechanisms—nozzles for dispensing knockout gas that can penetrate energy shields and solid matter; laser grids capable of dicing me into tiny cubes in a micro-second; paralyzing psyche wave emitters that would reduce me to a blithering imbecile.

I prepare to defend myself against them—hoping I and my skin suit are up to the challenge.

Yet as I pass, not one of them activates. If this is all a ruse, it's not a very good one. The lady-matons haven't tried to kill me once

—not so much as a tranquilizing pellet. I've never been more insulted in my life!

"You'll pay for this arrogance!" I shout.

Unless … if they can't be bothered with this weaponry, what they have waiting for me must be so much worse. Am I … excited? Is that the true reason I haven't rewound—because I *want* to see what Mairī Lin, I mean my enemy, has in store?

"Of course," I murmur, "so I can learn and steal from her then turn her own technology against her in another timeline."

Brilliant! That is *very* on-brand. I truly am the Timematician. Yes, I *will* steal that name too! Hahahahahaha!

I reach the center of The Asylum, armed and ready for the fight of my life. Above is a cracked concrete dome; below is Mairī Lin's army of orange, green, and purple lady-matons. Their remains litter the concrete floor. I lower my sidearm. The lady-matons have been blasted and torn apart.

There are hundreds of them. Some twitch and spark; others lie still. Phaser marks mar purple Dahomeys, which hold the arms and legs of green Gladyses and orange Saraswatis. This composition of *mortuus mechanica …*

"It's exquisite," I breathe.

In the middle of it all is the bait in the lady-maton trap—Mairī Lin's biological form, the one that somehow survived our death ray. Mairī Lin lies on a hovergurney; she's hooked up to a variety of sensors that hiss and beep.

It must be some sort of doomsday device! I thrill. Perhaps a matter rearranger. Oh, I hope! Or could it be something better? I can't wait to find out!

The squelch of my suited palms echoes dully, clapping slowly and dramatically as I fly over the railing and down into the atrium's depths. The hem of the archivist trench coat flutters around me as I mentally prepare to squash her in a battle for the ages.

I purposefully land in the middle of the battlefield, several measures away from Mairī Lin and her wicked contraption. I want to walk amidst the cybernetic carnage. The attention to detail is staggering; the way the lady-matons have fallen, it would fool a forensic investigator into believing a true faceoff took place. I know better, of course. This has all been staged—just like her big battle with her purple sister-selves was all for show so she could laugh in my face after yet another subterfuge.

"I suppose any moment now, your supposedly dismembered automatons will come to life and merge into a mega-maton," I say, stealing her of the pleasure of thinking she'll surprise me ever again. "Well, the drollery is on you. I've reclaimed my giant battle bot in low orbit. All I need do is snap my fingers, and it shall come crashing through that concrete dome, ready to tear your mega-maton to pieces."

A spark makes me swivel to my right, and I blast a legless, armless Gladys between her glasses. Her pulsing eyes go dark; the broken machines surrounding her make no move to join forces.

"I do love your sense for the spectacular," Mairī Lin says. I turn again but keep myself from shooting her decapitated pink head on the floor.

I step toward her slowly.

Any second now …

"This isn't a trap," the pink head says. "I've even disabled their self-destruct sequences."

I try to ignore her.

Oculi in prize, I remind myself. Eye on the prize.

I tread past the pink head. I'm within a few short measures of Mairī Lin's biological form. The hiss of an air compressor clicks on and off. Before I murder her, I take a moment to get a good look.

She's more emaciated than the *rosea machina* I've been battling, but otherwise, their facial features are identical. I was correct; she wanted to express herself through an homage to the blond actress, not become her. It would seem that desire extends to Mairī Lin's birth body. Her brown-skinned organic cheeks are tinted with rouge; her scalp is crested by a blond wig, and she wears a copy of the white dress I gave her, showing ribs and sternum where her cleavage would be if she weren't so gaunt.

A fan whirs to life, stirring the air, no doubt unleashing some sort of corrosive mist that will attack my suit. I wheel about, ready to blast the device, but the sound of Mairī Lin cooing makes me pause. The artificial wind makes her white dress flutter around her unmoving form, just like in one of the screenings she loves.

"Do you feel the breeze?" the pink lady-maton head asks, quoting her favorite actress. "Isn't it delicious?"

I pick the head off the floor, fix her blond hair, and place her on the bed. The fan whines; a belt breaks; the draft disappears; her fluttering dress collapses.

"Oh poo," Mairī Lin says in a pouty tone through the pink head. Her biological lips remain still.

She's paralyzed. That's no secret—Mairī Lin's infamous—but battling her lady-matons, and her intellect, to the death, made it easy to forget.

I doubt her biological body can bat an eye.

I step within the circle of tubes, compressed gas tanks, and cobbled-together battery packs surrounding her organic shell, which is far frailer than I'd ever have imagined. Only now do I see; what I took to be weapons of mass destruction is life-support equipment. A breathing tube is attached directly into her throat.

Within her sunken face, she gazes at me with large brown eyes that I momentarily don't look away from.

"It's nice to see you," she says, still speaking in that infernal seductive baby voice through the pink head.

"You're a fool," I reply.

My fingers curl around the breathing tube that runs into her throat. I give her time to think about what's about to happen.

"I'm already dying," she says. "Are you really in that much of a rush to be rid of me?"

I squeeze the tube. Her too-big eyes grow wider. A heart

monitor spikes. Her birth body gasps for air. Her metal head speaks unimpeded.

"I think you're the one person who can truly appreciate the irony. The genius of my über psyche was too great to transfer to a single lady-maton. So, I used four. That gave me the space I needed to move beyond my body. Then I built more hosts, more mechanical minds, and more storage capacity ... more than my biological brain could hold on its own. That allowed my intellect to grow even further. I was like a potted plant, finally free to spread my roots. But when my lady-matons destroyed each other, and all their, my, psyches downloaded back into my bio brain, the vastness I'd become was too much. I literally outsmarted myself."

I release the tube. Her breathing and heart rates stabilize.

What are you doing? I rage at myself. *Kill her, now, while you have the chance!*

And yet, what's the point of killing her when she's on the cusp of death?

"If this is another one of your tricks—" I warn.

"My silly Timematician," she sighs, sounding more tired than condescending. "I'm done with tricks and traps. I invited you here because I don't want to die alone."

The light of my social barometer swirls through a rainbow of colorful symbols and then winks out; despite numerous updates and recalibrations, when it comes to Mairī Lin, it's as lost as I am.

"Invited me here?" I snort, falling into the comfortable and ego-bolstering habit of bluster. "You were too busy fighting yourself to send coordinates. *I* found *you*!"

I stop. Truth silences me, and then it speaks. "You dropped the shielding on The Asylum so my sensors could detect your battle."

"It was Gladys' idea," the pink head explains.

I yank off my monocle and slam it against the floor.

"Why can't you let me have one victory?" I demand of her paralyzed form. "Just one!"

I pant, fists clenched. I try to glare at her, but I can't look her in her organic eyes. I stare at the pink head on the bed instead.

She sighs tiredly. "You've watched that precog rodent movie how many times, yet still you think winning is the opposite of losing. Sometimes you have to lose to win the greatest prize of them all."

"I suppose you're referring to yourself," I snort.

"Of course!" she thrills. "That, and love."

"Love?" I ask. "I don't believe in love."

"Such a terrible liar. Besides, a person may not believe in air, but they still need it to breathe. Did you ever finish watching the black and white screening about the two gender-morph musicians on the run from organized crime?"

"Of course not," I snort.

"Another fib," she tsks. "Shall we watch it now? Together?"

"Yes," I say before I can stop myself.

She's in your head, the Genetrix part of me warns, *when it's you who should be in hers.*

I sense one of Genetrix's trademark motherly tirades building. It would be so easy to give into it. Instead, I firmly reply, *Silentium.*

Chapter 18

I find a chair amidst the remains of Mairī Lin's lady-maton army, set it by her side, and sit. An automated drawer under her bed hisses open. I flinch, still suspecting a trap. If that's the case, it couldn't be delivered in a more delicious package.

Inside the drawer is a Twinkie in a clear wrapper on a gold plate next to a single-serve carton of milk.

"You like Twinkies?" I ask, wondering why she has one under her bed.

"I have no idea," the pink head answers. "I've never had one. But you love them. I didn't think this moment would ever come, but part of me hoped, so I saved it for you, just in case."

I savor the crackle as I open the wrapper, and the pink head projects a hologram of the antiquated screening she adores.

By the end of the opening act, as I wash the aftertaste of saccharine Twinkie coating the inside of my mouth with a swig of perfectly chilled milk, I almost believe Mairī Lin and I are having a genuine moment. When we get to the scene where the criminal kingpin executes his enemies, gangland-style, I avert my eyes and instinctively grab Mairī Lin's biological hand.

"Sorry," I say, releasing my grip. "I'm a genocidal maniac—"

"Same," Mairī Lin agrees.

"But that scene always bothers me."

"It's all right," she says. "It's nice to be touched by you. It makes me wish we were watching something full of assassinations."

I blink in confusion.

"So you'd never let me go," she patiently explains.

I reach for her, then hesitate. Another drawer hisses open under her bed. Inside is a bottle of disinfectant.

I'm still wearing my suit, so theoretically there's nothing to fear —other than the unknown. For comfort, I squirt and rub some antiseptic into her palms. She giggles because "it's cold," and then I tentatively curl my fingers around hers.

When the lead actress sings 'I'm Through with Love,' Mairī Lin and I sing along.

"You maniacal minstrel," she says when the song ends. My social-ometer may be useless with her mechanically modulated voice, but I'm confident she's teasing me in a friendly way.

"Madness is genius," I reply, "and it's better to be absolutely ridiculous—"

"Than absolutely boring," she finishes with me as we quote her favorite actress.

I gaze at her biological lips.

"The real lover is the man who can thrill you just by touching your head," I say, borrowing another line, "or smiling into your—"

"Kiss me," she says.

I look from her birth body to her lady-maton head.

"Which you?" I ask. Who am I to presume which form she most identifies with?

"The biological me," she answers.

Her words tug my heart in a way I've never felt; in a way I thought I would never feel; in a way I never would've thought I would give in to.

Before I second guess myself, I undo the coat from *The Archivist*

Wears Black, my polymer suit opens, and I step free. It's difficult to explain why I'm leaving the armor behind. Perhaps it's my sense of the dramatic.

If I'm going to do this, I want to do it right.

I wince as I put weight on my bum leg.

Beneath the battle garb, I'm dressed in my silk onesie. I don the archivist coat overtop.

This is her springing her trap! a part of me warns.

Whatever she has planned, I'm defenseless.

I am not Dr. BetterThan; I am just as stupid and banal as everyone else. In the end, she isn't beating me with technology, but by manipulating my emotions. I know it; I see it; I feel it, yet I'm a willing accomplice. I disgust myself the way humanity's stupidity disgusted me; simultaneously, I'm jealous, for this is how those lucky bastards got to feel daily. I brace myself; I've seen how this ends for others; I know how this will surely end for me—badly.

I move closer.

This is going to be the death of you! a part of me rages.

I know, I reply, calmer than I'd have imagined possible.

"So, this is your gambit," I say. "Using your feminine wiles to defeat me where your technology has failed."

Such are my words, but my voice trembles, devoid of its usual rancor.

"Kiss me, my silly Timematician," she replies.

At least use the defensive wax! a part of me shouts.

From my coat pocket, I remove a cylinder of chapstick, ostensibly for its anti-poison and antiseptic properties; in truth, the elements have not been kind to me, and I want to soften my cracked lips. A glance lets me see Mairī Lin's eyes twinkling like holiday lights as I apply the moisturizing substance.

"Me too, please," her pink head says.

I touch her paralyzed cheek and slowly draw the glossy wax stick across her lips, hoping I'm not too clumsy, then place the tube back in my pocket.

I lean over her, my mouth approaching hers. If she has a remaining Dahomey, she could easily shoot me in the back.

My mouth meets Mairī Lin's, soft and warm. Heat rushes through me—poison, no doubt, dosed through our epidermal contact, administering a venom too powerful for the enzymes in the wax to break down. I feel the effects of her toxin grow stronger; my heart expands, bigger and bigger, thudding against my ribcage as it readies to explode. What a way to go. And yet, my cardiovascular system keeps pumping, stronger and surer than before. A seed, long dormant in my chest, cracks open; it sprouts and grows, filling me with buoyant light. It's as if all things were possible—through my go-to roadmap of science and do-overs but also something more.

The logical part of me knows what this feeling is; it's a mix of phenylethylamine, adrenalin, norepinephrine, dopamine—

Shush, I tell the bullet list of "love" chemicals forming in my head.

I am the Timematician, but it's this kiss that makes the clock stop, coalescing past, future, and present into one.

I'm convinced this moment shall last forever—then a blaring alarm pulls me from perfection. It's Mairī Lin's heart-rate monitor falling flat. The drone fills my ears and my world. The warmth drains from her lips.

"Mairī Lin?" I ask. As the twinkle in her eyes fades, I'm able to meet her gaze; she stares lifelessly at the concrete dome above. "Mairī Lin!"

I cradle her small, frail body, rocking it gently.

"It's OK," I whisper. "I'm coming."

I grit my teeth, and my stomach churns as I throw my psyche back in time by a few minutes. I concentrate and land exactly where I want to be. Mairī Lin is alive, in my arms, and we are kissing anew. I'm lost in transcendence until I hear her heart monitor flatten once more. I rewind again, and again, and again. I don't wait for her to die to repeat the cycle. I lose myself in her kiss, entering an endless loop of perfection. This is how I shall remain, in this matchless moment, blissfully lost, forever. I will stretch this moment so thin, I'll erase myself with, dare I say it, love?

I'm close to infinity, which is the same as nothing—but I never reach it. Time jerks me into its normal flow. I'm still here, but Mairī Lin is gone—not dead in my arms, gone.

I blink in surprise and look around the cavernous chamber in the middle of The Asylum.

Above is the cracked concrete dome; around me are the battered remains of the fallen lady-matons; Mairī Lin and her medical equipment are nowhere to be seen.

My head throbs, my skin crawls, and I vomit. My first thought is she's poisoned me after all; perhaps, in a way, she has. This physical reaction is surely because she's changed the past. Every time I rewound to renew our lip lock, it released an echo. She's time-sensitive; she felt and saw our future kiss and took steps to make sure it never happened.

The realization is eclipsed by a blinding migraine unlike any pain I've known. I can guess the catalyst. In breaking the timeloop, Mairī Lin's created a paradox between what had been and what now is.

My brain and body struggle to meld together the altered sequence of this timeline with the one I left. I whimper and my bowels constrict as I process the dissonant memories that Mairī Lin has created in me by not being under the concrete dome when I arrive. They play like a point-of-view screening.

I "relive" this revised series of moments; in this new version, when I reach the railing above and look below, I never see Mairī Lin in the center of the defunct lady-matons because, in this version of events, Mairī Lin hid herself elsewhere. And so, when I stopped at the railing, I'm forced to recall, I spied Mairī Lin's pink lady-maton head in the middle of the cybernetic battlefield. Suspecting a trap, I flew down to spring it—which catches me up to the present; no more new memories are being shoved into me.

I look to the floor. Between my feet is her pink head, eyes dark.

167

Why did she end our eternal kiss? I wonder.

Because she sees you for the loser that you will always be, the Genetrix in me replies.

The expansion in my chest that ballooned the moment my lips met Mairī Lin's shrivels like rotting fruit discarded in the sun. Salty tears brim and overflow. I lift the pink head and smash it against the floor. The thing cracks, its eyes glow, and it projects a hologram of Mairī Lin in her white dress.

"Hello, my Timematician," she says.

"Where are you?" I hiss. "I'm going to kill you!"

"You're too late for that," she replies. "I'm already dead. This holo interface is programmed to respond in my place."

"Liar!" I snap. "You don't die for several more minutes."

"I changed that," she says, "to save you."

My hurt rage drains from me. I look into her holo eyes the way I couldn't her biological ones. My voice quivers and sticks as I struggle to respond. "But … I'm here to save you."

"I know," she says. Her hand reaches for my cheek and passes through. "No more do-overs; not for us."

"I *will* save you," I reply. "You can't stop me."

"I'm the one person who can," she answers.

"But why, if you love me—"

"*Because* I love you. You know the rules," she says. "They're *your* rules. No reliving this perfect moment. You'll either ruin it—"

"Or stretch it thin," I finish for her. "I don't care."

"I do," she replies. "Would you like to hear what I think?"

"No," I say.

"I think the only reason you planned to destroy the world was because you knew you could go back and save it," she says.

"Save it?" I scoff.

"I think parts of me always wanted you to," she says. "I think that held parts of me back when we fought. Deep down, I don't think I ever wanted you to die. I mean, I had to wait long enough to finally meet you."

I blink rapidly as I process her words. Tears come to my eyes. "I don't want you to die either."

"Too late," she says sadly. "You want a *real* challenge, my Timematician? Don't destroy this broken world. Fix it."

I wheeze a laugh. "You want me to save them? After the way they treated me? Treated you? You … want me to be a hero?"

"You *are* a hero," she replies. "My hero. You forgot you put your death ray on a timer; otherwise, I doubt you ever would've gone through with your genocidal plan."

I don't argue. "I don't think you could've done it either."

"You've met Dahomey. She is a part of me. You know I could go through with it. But that was before I met you. I want you to save yourself, and me, by saving them."

"They'll never accept me," I insist.

"Just find one," she says, "one person who needs a friend; be that friend to them. Use your power if you have to. Form that connection."

"That will never work," I insist.

"It did with us," she answers, "when I was a friend to you."

"You tried to kill me!"

"Parts of me did. And look at us now."

I'm silent. Her words are heavy.

"If I go back, do you think you'll remember me?" I ask. "With your déjà vu?"

"Maybe," she says. "But to do this right, you'll have to go deep into your past—to before you became a villain. And the further you go, the more events will diverge, bearing little to no resemblance to this timeline. My guess is any déjà vu I have will seem as passing, useless hallucinations."

"We'd be starting from scratch," I say.

"I would be," she concedes. "Obey your rules. Don't attempt to redo what we have. You can't. It's too twistedly, perfectly, special. You'll ruin it if you try."

"But—" I start to protest.

"Do you know what this mudra means?" she cuts me off. She touches the tips of her middle fingers and thumbs, pointing them toward her chest.

"Kalesvara," I reply. Time god.

"Goodbye, my Timematician," she smiles, "and good luck."

Her ultra-sophisticated interactive hologram fades.

"Wait!" I shout, grabbing futilely at the air.

She's gone.

Epilogue

To say that I go on a rampage is to compare a mosquito bite to a mutated two-headed shark attack. Encased in my rubberized bodysuit, cracked monocle, and the archivist trench coat, I use nature-bending tech to erupt volcanoes, stir up cyclones, and pulverize skyscrapers. In an ash-covered public square in Jupitar City, I point my wrist blaster at a domineering marble statue of muscled hero Captain Light.

I fire.

The statue splits then explodes; chunks smash against my floating form; the head lands in a pillow of ash.

None of it matters.

My black coat swirls around me as I touch down. I sit on Captain Light's strong jaw and cowled face. My mask opens and rolls back. I crack open a scavenged can of beer—beverage of the banal. My face squinches as I force the warm brew past my tongue. I crunch the empty can and throw it into a growing pile of its brethren. I open another.

Above me, the moon looms larger and larger, and not in a literary allusion kind of way. My armada of flying saucers attached rocket thrusters to the celestial body, pushing it out of its orbit and into the earth's atmosphere. The horizon blazes red.

"Resume screening," I order.

The city's emergency broadcast system shows a towering black and white hologram of a long-dead, busty blond actress. She dances in the passenger car of a train, shaking her bosom, playing the ukulele, and singing about not loving anybody.

The moon fractures above me, breaking into pieces; the chunks light the sky as they burn in the atmosphere. The larger fragments strike the planet's surface, making the ground shake. The impacts run deep; de-crystallizing the globe left it brittle. Cracks snake through the concrete at my feet. Molten lava bubbles up. The entire planet is coming undone.

"Just like my heart," I murmur. I recline on Captain Light's nose and gaze up at the projection.

The statue sinks, and lava flows between my feet, catching my archivist coat on fire. As I burn, I spread my arms and say goodbye to this broken world and broken life.

"*Nunc futuri*," I say miserably.

My innards lurch, and the moon returns to its orbit; the earth reforms, and my psyche flies backward, past my final conversation with Mairī Lin's hologram, traveling in reverse through The Asylum, disassembling my ad hoc master control panel in the comic book lair, and whooshing out of a hole in the store's ceiling that reseals as I'm suctioned into the storm clouds above.

The soles of my armor chase missiles in reverse before I reach the binge-watch marathon of the derogatory doctor and his bumbling bot; I don't dare pause. Back I go, now lurching through the epic battle I barely survived in Mairī Lin's crystal cavern. I note that the gems' quantum stabilization field seems only to affect me if they are present when I initiate a jump. Since they were not at my point of origin, I am like water passing through the sieve of these crystals past.

I reach and fly through my first encounter with Mairī Lin as her *machina rosa* stands within my ocean base reading my memoirs. I untype my great work, step backward into my birdcage elevator, then witness the death-ray blast that eviscerated humanity playing in reverse, seemingly restoring the population as the beam flies from the earth to the moon. In my laboratory, my nemesis with the bird insignia holds me down, then jumps back and out the wall she blew open. I go further still, decade after decade into my past, undoing, or more accurately, never doing, moment after moment of villainy.

I gain momentum as I dive deeper into the temporal anomaly in my brain, the one that somehow stores all these once-lived, never-to-bes. As I approach my desired destination, I overshoot my intended return gate by mere minutes—but what a difference a few minutes can make.

I'm no longer a man nor even a teenager, but on the verge of puberty.

I feel my adult psyche inhabit my school-boy self as he/we stand on the stage of an academic auditorium. I'm dressed in Valkyrie drag—blond wig, horned helm, tasseled spear—before an audience of parents, teachers, and fellow students. Until my kiss with Mairī Lin, this was the most perfect moment of my life, the moment when I showed the world my talent, and the world responded with a standing ovation and demands for an encore.

My mother was never prouder. I see her standing in the aisle with a refurbished digicam pointed at me. A rose broach glints on the lapel of her dress jacket. Her hair is styled in a beehive updo. I wear tinted glasses with audio mufflers to help me deal with the stage lights and harsh noises. Applause washes over me—in reverse. Through the audio filter, it's like the steady beat of waves—and so much more. They see and recognize my glory.

This is the moment when I feel whole; this is the moment that turns me into a villain as I desperately attempt to get that feeling back—a goal that is mocked and foiled by ingrates so many times I determine the only way to get it again is to rule the world.

As I rewind, they stop clapping, they sit, and back I go. The song I sang, the one that Mairī Lin played to lure me into her crystal cavern, returns down my throat and into my lungs.

I grit my teeth, grip the quantum reigns at last, and my innards lurch to a halt, shaking me to my cellular and psychic core as I plant myself shortly before my performance is to begin. I snap into place. Certain moments are magnetic like that.

I never thought I'd dare come back here. What if I get caught in another loop of singing perfection?

So be it, I think.

I open my mouth to repeat that glorious instance, to unleash the magnificent song stored in my belly, and I promptly throw up.

The thundering applause I remember experiencing is replaced by disgust, pity, and laughter; my mother lowers the camera, shaking her head in disappointment. The faux-jewel, rose-shaped broach pinned above her dress collar glints like a dagger. She touches her lacy cravat. I barely see or hear; I care even less.

I have senses only for the girl in the front row—a girl who was not here the first time this happened. I don't even know what borough she's from.

She's strapped into a battered wheelchair with dented rims. She's thin but nowhere near as gaunt as the woman I fell/fall in love with in a future that will never be. The face of the pubescent girl in this present is devoid of makeup; the permed blond wig I recall is not to be seen. Her biological hair is jet black and cut short. Instead of a billowy white dress that shows off non-existent cleavage, she's stuffed into an ill-fitting gray sweatshirt and pants. How she must hate them.

I struggle and fail to meet the gaze of her biological form, but from the periphery of my vision, I lose myself in her lips. They twitch, managing a smile. At this age, she isn't fully paralyzed. She mouths the word, *Hello.*

I wipe vomit from my cheek and lips.

She came for me.

My chest swells. I try to run for the stairs at the side of the stage so I can go to her, but my bum leg in an antiquated squeaky brace trips me. I'd forgotten how heavy it is. I grunt as my knee hits the stage. I lift my hand to wave to her, but red stage curtains slam in front of me.

"Stagefright sucks, am I right?" asks gymnast Trey Chakrabarti. His stupid shirtless, smooth muscles flex and glint with baby oil. Behind him is a giant hanging canvas with the cautionary/prodding message, DON'T BE DNA REGULAR. BE GEN M.

He offers his hand to help me up. I push it away, struggle to my feet, and fumble my way through the curtain's thick fabric. On the other side, Mother is gone. I'll have to make my own way home; I'd blocked out what that's like. The audience disperses, muttering about the gimpy fat boy who ruined the finale. I can't be bothered with thoughts of how I will destroy them one by one.

"Mairī Lin?" I call. "Mairī Lin!"

I see someone, Mairī Lin's father, I presume, rolling her out an exit. The chase is on. I hobble stage right, down a short set of stairs. I can catch her, and when I do—

A stout girl steps firmly in my way. She wears a worn t-shirt with the graphic of a shadowren on it, wings spread, and she holds a plastic sword under one arm. It takes me a moment to recognize her. It's hard to believe that this clod will (may) one day yield a katana that can cut through anything.

"Stand aside!" I shout. I try to sound imperious, but it comes out nasally and whiny.

"These are for you," she says, thrusting a bouquet of plastic roses into my arms. The red petals are worn and faded, undoubtedly salvaged from a recyclage plant. The would-be katana girl gruffly brushes past.

"Ow!" I yelp.

"Thanks for barfing," she mutters as she heads for the prop room. "I guess I'll be the one to clean it up."

I'm about to throw the flowers at her uncaring back when I notice the card attached to the artificial bouquet. Thoughts of retribution dissolve as I numbly pull the horned helm and blond wig from my scalp; I drop them to the tile floor. A single word is written on the envelope:

TIMEMATICIAN

I know that font.

My hands tremble as I rip open the envelope and yank free a simple card; the stock appears to be home-pressed paper with embossed butterflies. On one side is a crayon drawing of a pink lady-maton with blond hair; she holds the hand of a figure in a long black military-style coat and a form-fitting mask with a monocle. I turn the card over.

To futures that will never be, it reads in a feminine, curly-cue typeset. *Nunc futuri. MLM* 💋

I smile and rub tears from my eyes. I gaze at the red imprint from her perfect kiss and press it to my lips.

For the first time in many lifetimes, I don't know what to do.

Do I follow my own rules and let her go?

Do I go after her?

Do I destroy the world … or do I try to save it?

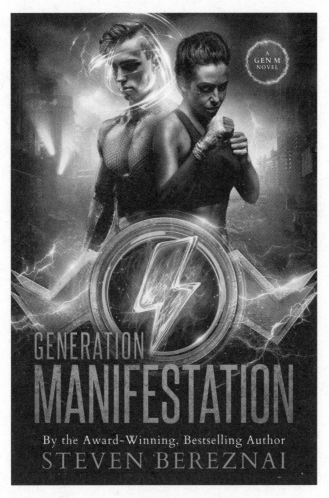

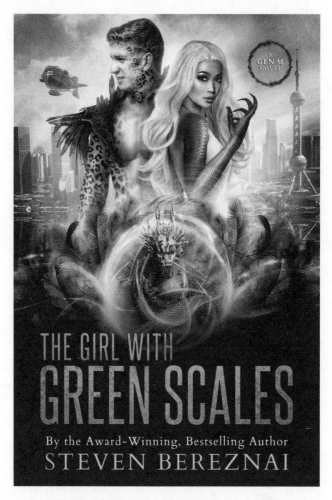

THE GIRL WITH GREEN SCALES

By the Award-Winning, Bestselling Author
STEVEN BEREZNAI

Want to know more about Mairī Lin's future?

Order *The Girl With Green Scales* today!

www.GenerationManifestation.com

Author Afterthoughts

Hello, Reader :)

Thank you for taking the time to read *The Timematician*.

As with any book, much thought, sweat, tears, and smiles went into writing this. I won't say that I got it all right; I hope I got more right than wrong.

If you enjoyed this tale, please take a moment to write a review on your favorite retailer site and **Goodreads.com**. This helps a lot! Also consider buying a copy as a gift.

I'm hard at work on more books in the *Gen M* series as I strive to turn it into a fully formed universe, one book at a time. The more positive and insightful feedback I get, the more I'll know people are interested, and the quicker I'll get them done.

As The Timematician would say, *Nunc futuri*.

Also by Steven Bereznai

Generation Manifestation (A Gen M Story: Book 1)

The Girl With Green Scales (A Gen M Story: Book 3)

Queeroes

Queeroes 2

How A Loser Like Me Survived the Zombie Apocalypse

The Adventures of Philippe and the Outside World

The Adventures of Philippe and the Swirling Vortex

The Adventures of Philippe and the Hailstorm

The Adventures of Philippe and the Big City

The Adventures of Philippe and the Magic Spell

Gay and Single…Forever?—10 Things Every Gay Guy Looking for Love (and Not Finding It) Needs to Know

About the Author

In grade two, I wrote a not-so-breathtaking poem for my school's literary anthology. I've been a writer ever since. My experience includes writing/producing for CBC TV, a short film and reality stint at OUTtv, and penning some award-winning, bestselling novels.

I came out in my late teens and feeling like an outsider has deeply impacted my sensibility. I love writing that combines sass, heart, speculative fiction, and (where appropriate) abs. Basically, shows like *Buffy*, *Teen Wolf* and *She-Ra and the Princesses of Power*.

I'm Toronto-based and can be reached through my website www.stevenbereznai.com.

Shadowren

Comic books were a big part of my teen years and
have continued to influence my aesthetics. No
wonder they provided lots of inspiration for
Generation Manifestation: A Gen M Novel Book 1. I
couldn't resist doing a mock cover for one of the
comic books that appears in the novel.

Release the kraken

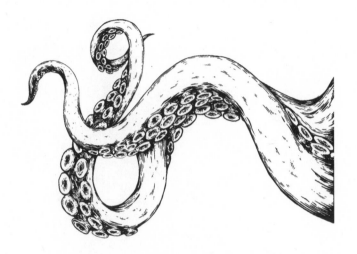

In *The Girl With Green Scales*, I'm super excited to introduce readers to more parts of the world our Gen M heroes (and villains!) are growing up in. You'll learn about the high-society socialistas (and the important role they serve), travel to retro-futuristic Jupitar Island, and maybe even meet a kraken :)